STARRY, STARRY NIGHT

Childhood friends and cousins Leo and Alice had imagined their whole lives playing out on their beloved Devon beach. But one night, sitting on the sand beneath the stars, Alice tells Leo a secret that must never be shared, then packs her bag and flees.

Leo is left to build his own life. He surrounds himself with other family and friends and is content on the whole. But he is left with a sense of what — or who — is missing. So decades later, when he receives a note from Alice asking if she can come home, he doesn't hesitate to agree.

But as the stars align and their reunion draws near, Leo is left to consider their separation and what so many years apart means for a relationship solidified in youth and a secret which could affect the whole family.

THE ULVERSCROFT FOUNDATION
(registered UK charity number 264873)

was established in 1972 to provide funds for research, diagnosis and treatment of eye diseases. Examples of major projects funded by the Ulverscroft Foundation are:-

- The Children's Eye Unit at Moorfields Eye Hospital, London
- The Ulverscroft Children's Eye Unit at Great Ormond Street Hospital for Sick Children
- Funding research into eye diseases and treatment at the Department of Ophthalmology, University of Leicester
- The Ulverscroft Vision Research Group, Institute of Child Health
- Twin operating theatres at the Western Ophthalmic Hospital, London
- The Chair of Ophthalmology at the Royal Australian College of Ophthalmologists

You can help further the work of the Foundation by making a donation or leaving a legacy. Every contribution is gratefully received. If you would like to help support the Foundation or require further information, please contact:

THE ULVERSCROFT FOUNDATION
The Green, Bradgate Road, Anstey
Leicester LE7 7FU, England
Tel: (0116) 236 4325

website: www.ulverscroft-foundation.org.uk

MARCIA WILLETT

♦

STARRY, STARRY NIGHT

Complete and Unabridged

LARGE
PRINT

ISIS
Leicester

First published in Great Britain in 2021 by
Bantam Press
an imprint of
Transworld Publishers
London

First Isis Edition
published 2021
by arrangement with
Transworld Publishers
Penguin Random House UK
London

A catalogue record for this book is available
from the British Library.

ISBN 978–1–78541–999–7

Published by
Ulverscroft Limited
Anstey, Leicestershire

Printed and bound in Great Britain by
TJ Books Ltd., Padstow, Cornwall

This book is printed on acid-free paper

To Joanna

PART ONE

PART ONE

1

Leo stands at his study window, watching the familiar scene: rabbits racing across the field, disappearing amongst tall grasses in the ditch beneath the blackthorn hedge, and, beyond the field, the silvery water of Slapton Ley shimmering amongst the reedbeds. Far out to sea, the sun balances briefly on the horizon before rising into the clear sky.

He picks up the mug of coffee from the windowsill, warming his hands around it, taking a sip. As he listens to Jazz FM — Chet Baker singing 'My Funny Valentine' — his eyes are fixed on the tranquil rural landscape, but he is seeing something quite different: a scene acted out on a summer's afternoon more than forty years ago, beyond this window in the garden; his sisters carrying the tea things, setting them on the table beneath the hawthorn tree, discussing the wedding plans. He remembers that, as he followed them, their cousin Alice came slipping out of the house behind them, drawing him aside.

'Something terrible has happened, Lion,' she said, clutching his arm, her eyes dark with anxiety. 'Can we go somewhere and talk? Can we go down to the beach?'

The use of the silly childish name distracted him from the pre-celebratory atmosphere that pervaded all their lives just then and he focused his attention on her. She'd arrived the previous evening, too late to have a catch-up chat, but now she had the wide-eyed, immobile expression of someone who had sustained a

3

shock. Instinctively he turned her slightly away from his sisters.

'What's the matter?'

'I can't tell you here.'

As she looked beyond his shoulder to Margaret and Helen at the table, he experienced a mixture of irritation, concern and anxiety. Much as he loved Alice — and he loved her very much — nothing must be allowed to upset Helen's big day tomorrow. From childhood upward, Alice's tendency for drama, for hamming it up, was an accepted part of her character. Allowances were made when she was small because her mother had died whilst she was still a baby, and her soldier father was away a great deal of the time, but Leo had realized a long while since that Alice's instinct to amuse was very often an effort to mask her sense of inadequacy: making people laugh often inspires affection, diverts anger. As a child Alice had been parcelled out to relatives for most of the school holidays but her happiest times had been spent here in the old stone house above Start Bay with her aunt and uncle and cousins at Long Orchard. Now the cousins were grown up and tomorrow Alice was to be one of Helen's bridesmaids.

'What's the problem?' Leo asked, edging her towards the corner of the house, into the shadow, keeping his voice cheerful in an effort to defuse any tendency towards dramatics. 'Don't tell me you've put on weight and the dress doesn't fit?'

'Yes,' she answered flatly. 'Exactly that. Oh God, Lion. I'm pregnant.'

He glanced instinctively at the happy group by the table, his immediate, overriding reaction one of fear lest his sister's wedding day should be in any way

4

spoiled — and Alice saw this in his face and drew back from him at once. It was as if he had struck her, rejecting all the closeness and love built between them through the years of childhood and growing up.

'Hang on, Al,' he said quickly, trying to regain ground, stretching out a hand to her, but Mags was calling to them — 'Come on, you two, your tea is getting cold' — and Alice pushed past him and crossed the grass to the garden table under the hawthorn tree. He could hear her voice, light, amused, and he knew that he had failed her.

It was early evening before he could talk to her again, tracking her down to the garden-room where cut flowers filled every available vase and jug, and Helen's voice, always louder than anyone else's, was detailing off decorating parties to carry them down to the church. Leo seized Alice by the hand and dragged her out into the stone-flagged passageway between the kitchen and the garden-room.

'What about that walk down to the sea?'

'Oh, no,' she protested. 'We should be helping.' But he could see that she longed to go; to escape.

'They don't need us,' he said. 'Helen's got everyone organized. Come on.'

They hurried away, crossing the garden, out into the lane and down to the village. Passing over the slipway between the hotel and the café and on to the beach, they continued to walk until they reached the sea's edge. The tide was on the turn, the sea resting placidly against the shore, and they sat down together on the sun-warmed stones.

'So,' he said at last. 'Do you want to tell me about it?'

Alice crossed her ankles, drew up her knees and

folded her arms around them. She was wearing a long wrap-around indigo-blue Indian cotton skirt and a T-shirt. Her plaited brown hair reached nearly to her waist.

'Yes,' she said. 'And no. As soon as I saw you I wanted to blurt it all out but now I don't know where to begin. It's all so terrible and . . . and unmanageable.'

He sensed her panic and felt his own fear rising again. It was essential to remain calm and sympathetic.

'Start at the beginning, go on till the end, then stop,' he said, glancing at her. 'You're pregnant. Are you absolutely sure?'

Her profile was so set, so still, that he reached out to touch her hand, and she smiled briefly. As their eyes met, just in that moment, he knew that she was wondering whether to retract: to take the opportunity he'd given her to say that she wasn't sure, that she might be panicking. Part of him wanted her to say that, to let him off the hook, but his affection for her reached out to her fear.

'Tell me,' he said almost angrily.

She shook off his hand and dropped her forehead on to her knees.

'Yes,' she muttered. 'I'm sure.'

'Who's the father?'

Alice clasped her knees more tightly, pressing her face against them so that her voice was muffled.

'George,' she muttered. 'It's George. Oh God, Lion, what am I going to do?'

* * *

6

Leo swallows his coffee and turns away from the window. The failures and humiliations of our pasts remain as fresh and sharp in our hearts as eggshells newly cast on to a compost heap. What should he have said to her? What solution was there to such a problem? His little cousin, one of the people he loved best in all the world, was pregnant with the child of his about-to-be brother-in-law. Leo was not quite twenty-one, ready to start his final year at the Royal Agricultural College, Cirencester and his experience of life was limited.

He can remember her long skirt making a puddle of indigo on the stones, the fine gold chain around one of her thin ankles, the misery in her brown eyes. But he can't remember how he answered her. And now he has this letter from her. His fingers close over it, crumpling it, but the words are in his head: 'Dear Lion, May I come home . . . ?'

Impulsively, he thrusts the letter into the pocket of his cords, takes his coffee mug into the kitchen and puts it on the long refectory table. The kitchen is big, with a raftered ceiling and slate-flagged floor. It's still much as it was when his parents were here: the Belfast sink and wooden draining boards; the cream Aga; the built-in dresser with its variety of mis-matched china and pottery all anyhow along the shelves.

His wife, Jenny, had never been very interested in the house, or in his plans for an arboretum and a wildflower meadow on the few acres on the hill above. She was a town mouse to his country mouse and it hadn't taken too long to realize that. After the initial passion was extinguished, there was very little to hold them together, apart from a very special friendship that neither wished to see destroyed. They separated amicably, agreeing that to waste money on divorce was foolish, and they still spend happy times together; she with him at Long Orchard, and he with her at her London flat. It works very well.

Leo makes porridge, eats it standing up, leaning against the Aga, his thoughts still back in a summer long ago. Presently he goes into the passage, laces up his walking boots and takes his jacket from the peg. He lets himself out into the lane, closes the five-bar gate behind him and walks down to the village just as he and Alice walked on that hot summer's day all those years ago. Today the dazzling sky is almost Mediterranean blue and the early May sunshine is warm.

As he strolls across the slipway between the café and the hotel, which has been converted long since into holiday apartments, Leo can imagine Alice beside him in her long skirt, her gold-brown hair in a thick plait threaded through with ribbon. Very seventies: very what would now be called boho.

He stands by the sea wall, gazing at the panoramic beauty of the bay: from Start Point lighthouse on its rocky outpost to the west and across to the entrance to the River Dart at the eastern point. Tall grey cliffs, sheltered coves, small steep fields — Leo has lived out of this landscape for all of his life and he loves it. He knows that the sea, so silky-smooth today, can destroy walls, devastate villages, chew up roads. From his safe vantage point above Torcross he's watched with horror and awe as the easterly gales and high tides batter his friends' houses along the seafront; he's seen properties evacuated, windows broken by the stones flung by fast-travelling walls of white water, the road smashed. But somehow the village survives: properties are restored, the road rebuilt; life continues. He cannot imagine living anywhere else.

Now he stands watching the sea birds; a trawler heading for Brixham. He pushes his hands into his trouser pockets, his fingers encounter her letter and he pulls it out, squinting against the sun.

Dear Leo,
May I come home again? I saw someone the other day who told me that you are still at Long Orchard. I couldn't imagine you anywhere else.
Alice x

There is no address, merely a mobile phone number. He's already phoned the number but there is no answer and no voicemail asking him to leave a message. Still in shock at hearing from her, he simply switched the phone off and now he is here in the place where he was last alone with her, and he's feeling a different mix of emotions: guilt, relief, apprehension. She disappeared so neatly and completely from their lives.

'She said a friend phoned,' her father said, the morning after the wedding, 'and she hitched a lift to Totnes with one of the guests to catch the train back to town.'

To the brigadier, London was still 'town' back then. He was undisturbed by his daughter's behaviour. Everyone knew that Alice was very much of her generation: hitch-hiking, festivals, communes. She came and went at will: now here, now there. This vanishing away was typical of Alice, but Leo was still anxious.

'Did she leave a message, Uncle Philip?'

The brigadier shook his head. 'She'll be in touch,' he said confidently.

9

Leo walks down the steps that have replaced the slipway and begins to stroll along the beach. It was a crazy day, the wedding day, too busy for anything but an occasional quick glance at his cousin: a brief exchange. It wasn't true that her dress didn't fit — he guessed that his question had been so apt that she couldn't resist the sharp response — but he didn't doubt that she'd told him the truth. He wasn't even particularly surprised about George. He and Alice had known each other from childhood; it was Alice who introduced George to Helen. They were military children, sent away to school at a young age, used to separation from their fathers, and it had drawn them close, despite the fact that George was five years older.

'Does George know?' he asked, back then, that evening on the beach.

'Good grief, no!' she said, her face frantic. 'How can I possibly tell him now? Anyway, I don't want him or Helen to know. It was just one of those crazy one-off moments. I was having a downer and he was having a sudden fit of nerves about the wedding. You know?'

And then they heard someone calling. Mags was hurrying down to them.

'Everyone's wondering where you've gone. Trust you to skive off. Come on, there's so much to do.' And they turned back with her. No further conversation was possible.

Afterwards, Leo tried to find Alice — phoning her friends, following clues as to her whereabouts — but she continued to elude him through that long hot summer until her father informed the family that she and a friend had gone to Italy on a cultural exchange her college of art was organizing. Leo asked for her address, wrote to it, and received a postcard in return:

10

'I'm fine, old Lion. Don't worry about me. Love you. Alice xx'.

This was the pattern of the years ahead. He stayed in touch through his uncle, who was not a very satisfactory correspondent: Alice was abroad . . . working as a chalet girl . . . had a job in an art gallery in Fiesole . . . was at a commune in Wales. There was no mention of a child. Uncle Philip retired from the army and married again, a confident, energetic widow with a family of her own. Mags got married, Helen had a baby, Leo met Jenny — life was busy. Then Uncle Philip died.

'Apparently,' Helen murmured to Leo at the funeral, 'they couldn't track Alice down. She turns up unexpectedly from time to time but she hasn't been in touch for ages. Mind you, I don't altogether blame her. Pushed from pillar to post all through her childhood, and then the ghastly Agnes as a stepmother, not to mention those two awful boys she brought along with her. Poor old Alice never stood a chance. I just wish I knew she was OK.'

Leo felt the sharp, eggshell stab of guilt. He glanced at George, still handsome in that rumpled, man-child way, and George looked back at him with a kind of rueful half-shrug.

'She was always a bird of passage, our Alice, wasn't she?' George remarked. 'Here today, gone tomorrow. Always someone else's horizon. We lost touch after Helen and I got married.'

'I still feel badly about it,' said Helen. 'We should have kept up somehow. She was such a funny child. Always laughing and joking but she must have been very lonely.'

Remembering, Leo instinctively pulls out his phone,

11

checks the number Alice has sent him and begins to text:

Of course you can come home. About time too. Leo x

He hesitates before he presses Send. As usual, his indecisiveness begins to erode that confident instinct to respond. Even as he hesitates he hears his name called and he turns, thrusting his phone into his pocket, the text unsent. A tall, elderly woman stands by the sea wall, waving to him.

'Hi, Bea.' He crunches across the shingle towards her. 'How are you doing? You're out early.'

'I could say the same to you,' she answers, and he has to prevent himself from explaining why he is out on the beach so soon after breakfast.

Bea Holmes always has this effect on him. She still has aspects of the prep school matron she was twenty years ago and Leo resists the urge to comb his fingers through his hair and pull his jersey straight.

'It's such an amazing morning,' he says, smiling at her. 'I simply couldn't help myself. What's your excuse?'

'Off to Dartmouth,' she answers. 'We like to get in early because of the parking. But I couldn't resist a quick stroll in the sunshine.'

'It'll be blowing a gale and pouring with rain next week,' he says.

'*Carpe diem*,' she agrees. 'Is all well?'

'Yes,' he answers quickly, too quickly, wondering if it's thirty years spent with small boys that gives her an unerring sense of something being not quite right. 'Everyone's fine. You must come and see the garden.

The wildflower meadow is beginning to look really good.'

'I'd like that. I'll be on my way, then.'

She raises a hand and turns to go. He watches her, then reaches into his pocket, feeling for his phone. He stares at the message he's typed but somehow he's lost his confidence; he's not certain if he should send it. Quickly he deletes it and turns back, walking quickly, heading for home.

2

Bea crosses the road and climbs back into the car. Her cousin, Will, sits hunched in the passenger seat, gazing out over Slapton Ley, waiting patiently. He's recovering from a hip replacement and is keeping walking to a minimum.

'Feel better for that?' he asks.

Bea fits the key into the ignition and nods as she starts the engine, backs out and turns the car towards Dartmouth.

'Yes, it's a beautiful morning for a walk. I saw Leo. Clearly he had the same idea.'

'He's up early. All well?'

Bea frowns. 'He looked furtive,' she says, after a moment.

Will is amused. 'In what way furtive? Doesn't sound like Leo.'

She gives a little shrug. 'Just a feeling.'

'Come on, Sherlock,' he says. 'You can do better than that. Was he wearing odd shoes? Trousers on back to front?'

'Very droll,' she answers. 'No. He was looking at his phone and then, when he saw me, he thrust it into his pocket very quickly. Almost guiltily.'

Will glances sideways at her. Bea has made no concession to the warm sunny morning. She wears cords, a warm jersey, and a padded gilet: she doesn't trust an English spring. They've lived together for more than twenty years now, ever since they and a much younger cousin, Tessa, inherited the old house and cottage in a

14

small cove just around the coast from Torcross. Neither Will nor Bea nor Tessa had ever met each other or their beneficiary, but they each decided to make a go of it together, and to their delight and mutual satisfaction the miracle worked. Tessa and Giles brought up their two children in the cottage with its boathouse converted into a photographic studio for Giles, whilst Will and Bea lived in the old stone house, which, in Will's view, was still inhabited by the spirit of their eccentric but benevolent cousin Mathilda Rainbird.

Will settles back into his seat and looks out at the Ley: at the mallard and coot busy in the rushes, the swans sailing serenely on the marshy waters. It's three years now since it was very reluctantly agreed that with worsening weather conditions and the erosion of beaches and cliffs, it would be sensible to sell up in the cove and move inland. They were lucky to find a buyer who intended to use the cottage and house as holiday lets, though they were heartbroken to leave the cove. A year ago this road across which they are passing was destroyed by a combination of easterly gales and huge seas. More properties were damaged and all four of them know they made the right decision, but Will can understand why, on a morning like this, Bea wants to stop the car and walk out to the beach.

'So,' he says, more to distract himself from sad thoughts rather than out of any real curiosity, 'old Leo's being furtive, is he? Perhaps we should invite him for a drink. It would do Tessa good to have a little party. I think she's a bit lonely now both the kids are at uni and Giles has gone on this assignment. And she's found moving away from the cove the hardest of all of us.'

15

As Bea turns the car inland, up the steep hill towards Strete, Will thinks with compassion of Tessa: of how, when she was only eleven and at boarding school, her parents and small brother were gassed to death when a volcano erupted in Cameroon, where her father was working as a petrochemical consultant. The cottage in the cove was her first real home since the disaster, her children grew up there, and she fought hard against leaving it.

'Why are you looking so glum?' demands Bea. 'Stop worrying and look out there. See the bluebells? And stop slouching. It's not doing your hip any good, sitting like that.'

Will grins and straightens his back, allowing himself only a tiny exclamation of discomfort, lest Bea should insist he stay in the car when they get to Dartmouth. He's looking forward to walking along the Embankment, seeing the boats on the river, listening to the gulls. He feels grateful for these last twenty years with his new-found family. Widowed, with no children, contemplating early retirement, he viewed this unexpected legacy as a kind of miracle. He was first attracted to his wife by her calm, blonde beauty, her smiling, good-natured charm, but later — too late — he discovered that it masked an unthinking indifference to life. Their only child was stillborn and his last hopes of happiness died with it. When he found himself amongst a group of delightfully unusual people who seemed to value him, to want to make a home with him, it was a new and wonderful experience.

'Leo invited us to see the wildflower meadow,' Bea is saying. 'Tessa would enjoy that. She needs some kind of occupation. These odd jobs she takes are all very well but she needs something to concentrate the mind.'

16

Will knows that Bea is right. He tries to imagine what warm-hearted, generous Tessa might do to distract herself from empty-nest syndrome, and the wrench of moving.

Bea is driving down College Hill and on to the Embankment. She pulls into a parking space.

'Excellent,' she says. 'You can have your walk and then head over to the Royal Castle. I'll meet you there for coffee when I've done some shopping.'

Will gets out carefully, balances himself and clasps his stick tightly. Here by the river there is a chill little breeze and, despite the sunshine, he is glad of the jacket Bea insisted he put on earlier.

'Sounds good to me,' he answers, and turns his attention to the river, sparkling, busy in the warm spring sunshine.

★ ★ ★

Bea walks away, glancing back briefly to check that Will is still upright, pleased to have parked so conveniently between the river and the Royal Castle, as well as having two hours' free parking into the bargain. Mentally she checks her shopping list, deciding where to go first: Boots the chemist, to get Will's prescription.

As she walks around the boat float, Bea sends up a little prayer of thanks for Will's recovery from the operation. She manages to conceal her anxieties about him, her fear that he might fall in his stubborn attempts to do too much too quickly. Her love for him threatens sometimes to overwhelm her: he is so dear to her. His companionship is so precious. She's seen how relationships deteriorate into a kind of

17

affectionate contempt, how love mutates into tolerant indifference. But she and Will share something different. Because there has never been passion between them there is no disillusionment. They accept each other, both aware of their good fortune.

They know how lucky they've been to have Giles and Tessa and their children as a close part of their lives: Charlotte and Henry are almost like their own grandchildren. Bea knows that Will is right when he says that Tessa has suffered most in the move. She insisted that they should not separate, refused to consider Bea and Will's suggestion that they should look for a place of their own. Apart from the financial considerations of buying two properties, Tessa was shocked that they should even think of it.

'We're a family,' she protested. 'We should stay together. Especially . . . '

She hesitated but Bea knew what she was thinking: that Will and Bea were getting old. Will quickly stepped in to cover the awkwardness, saying that it might be a problem to find a suitable property for such an odd group, but Tessa and Giles insisted that they'd find something that would work for them all. It took time and they had to compromise. The beach was no longer on their doorstep but they could see the sea from the upper windows and from certain points in the garden. The pretty stone house gave Tessa and Giles more room than they'd had in the cottage but the annexe was only just big enough for Bea and Will.

'But,' said Will, positive as always, 'no more stairs! That's definitely a bonus.'

And now, thinks Bea, given the hip operation it's a real blessing.

Nevertheless, it's good to go to the beach, to gaze

out at the sea and listen to its music. She thinks about Leo, standing by the great boulders brought in to strengthen the sea wall, staring down at his phone, and his expression as he turned to look at her. It was odd to see the normally calm, unemotional Leo looking so preoccupied, anxious; hastily pushing his phone into his pocket. It was as if she'd caught him in the middle of some misdemeanour — which is, of course, ridiculous. Bea takes the prescription, smiles at the pharmacist and heads out for the Co-op.

★ ★ ★

High up in the small apartment at the top of one of the old houses behind the church of St Saviour's, Emily Maybury stands on tiptoe to see out of the window that frames a glimpse of Bayards Cove, the moorings on the river and the harbour entrance. Soon she will walk to the café for her morning coffee but first she must finish her email to her best friend, Bethany. She sits down again at the table, opens her laptop and rereads what she has written so far.

Honestly, Bets, I just can't begin to thank your mum and dad enough for letting me have this amazing place while I try to get my ideas together. I know everyone thinks it's a bit crazy to be taking a sabbatical to try to write a radio play but everyone thinks I'm crazy anyway — actor father, opera singer mother, dysfunctional childhood — but, hey, I just know that I'm on to something here. And anyway, it's great to have some time off from the agency. I've got a really good idea for the play and I'm hoping to work it up into something. More about that later.

Em hesitates, then begins to type again.

I have to say straight off that I utterly love your pa-in-law. Wasn't last weekend just perfect? Thanks for inviting me over and introducing me to Leo. He was so sweet with your littlies and it's clear that he adores you and James. Isn't James like him? I love it that you all get on so well. Can't imagine him with Jenny, though! However did that happen? Not surprised that they separated. I mean, she's OK and all that, but she's such an old know-it-all, and I resented it when she said that my darling old dad was a terrible luvvie and that my family was like something out of Nancy Mitford. At least, I did until I read *Love in a Cold Climate* and then I realized that, unintentionally, it was the biggest compliment ever!

Anyway, Leo has invited me over for lunch on Friday! Can't wait! Meanwhile I shall go to the coffee house in Bayards Cove Inn and think about my play. It's a great place to sit and write and feel inspired — and that's not just because the owner, Charlie, is rather gorgeous.

Hugs to you all, Em xxxx

She sends the email, switches off the laptop and puts it into the brightly coloured woven shoulder-bag hanging on the chair. Bethany's parents let this apartment to visitors through the summer months, except for the week of the Regatta, when it's kept for family. It's neat and simple but delightfully shabby chic with its distressed, green-painted pine table and wicker chairs in the kitchen-living-room, only one double bedroom, with a tall, narrow cupboard and a painted chest, and a small shower-room. Nothing matches but everything lives together in harmony. Em knows how lucky she is to be here for these next few weeks and she intends to make the most of it. Bethany's mum has even arranged for one of their friends to give room to Em's old VW Golf on their driveway so that she has freedom to explore. She knows that she must work but this is such a magical place that she can't resist her little jaunts in the car.

It was good last weekend to go to Torcross, to meet Leo, whilst his son James, and Bethany and the children were staying. Bethany's mother-in-law, Jenny, lives in London, as do Em and Bethany, and just occasionally Em's been invited to a family party, but she'd never met Leo until now. She's rather surprised at how much she likes him. Definitely a silver fox: not tall but in very good shape, tanned and fit. She likes his quiet, gentle ways, shot through with sudden sharp humour, and the way he really listens when people are talking to him. He cooked a very good lunch and then they all walked to the beach. She can't remember when she's enjoyed herself so much.

Em frowns, slightly shocked about how she's feeling about James's dad, and glances through the high window at the clear blue sky. It looks heavenly but she'd learned that there can often be a chill breeze off the river, so she opens the painted cupboard in the bedroom and takes out her grey wool cardi-coat with its warm hood and slips it on, using both hands to wind her long fair hair more firmly into its knot. She picks up the shoulder-bag and lets herself out, locking the front door, putting the keys in her jeans

21

pocket, and running down the three flights of stairs. Outside she stands for a moment, looking up at the old church, studying the medieval houses, then she sets off through the narrow streets to Bayards Cove.

Before she goes into the elegant old Tudor inn, she walks on to the little quay to look out towards the castle at the mouth of the Dart and across the river to Kingswear, basking in the sunshine. An elderly man is also enjoying the scene, leaning on his stick, watching the cars driving off the ferry, glancing upwards at a noisy gull swooping over his head. They exchange a smiling glance that embraces the beauty of this magical spring morning and Em turns back and crosses the quay to the café. She pauses for a moment to adjust her sight from the brilliance of the sunshine and the dazzle of the river outside to the intimacy of low beams, reflected light from the bottles and glasses in the bar, and from the mirrors on the whitewashed walls. She is pleased to see that her favourite table in the alcove is empty. Smiling at the girl behind the bar, Em crosses between the tables and puts down her bag so as to guard her space against any incomers. She takes out her purse and goes to order a mocha.

Back at her table, she opens her laptop and finds her notes. She knows what she wants to achieve but isn't quite sure how she is going to do it. Since it is to be a radio play there can be no description, no narrative: only the characters can convey the story. There can be noises off: the hiss of the coffee machines, the clink of glasses and murmur of voices, but for the rest she must rely on dialogue and good actors — and a story.

Em looks around her. What she hopes to find in her own café scene is a link between the customers and the people who work there; something more than the familiarity of the regulars and the baristas, but what? She settles down, hoping that she's looking efficient, sips her mocha and waits for inspiration.

3

As soon as Bea and Will have driven away, Tessa regrets that she refused the chance of a lift to Dartmouth. Although they lead independent lives there's an unspoken agreement between the two households to offer a lift into the town. It's not that she needs any shopping but she would have enjoyed the company. Since they left the cove she's been battling with an odd mix of emotions: a sense of loss, of inertia — which has increased since both Henry and Charlotte are now away at university — and resentment. She didn't want to leave the cove, she would have taken her chances with the elements, but the opposition was too strong. Even Will, who loved it so much, believed that it was a sensible decision. The odd thing is that this act of leaving has reopened the old pain of bereavement, the loss of her parents and her little brother in that terrible disaster, and she finds that she is grieving at unexpected moments, reliving the anguish. She tries to rationalize it, to deal with it, but sometimes it's just too strong and it frightens her.

Giles is kind, understanding, because it is his nature to be so, but he's not really connecting with this at the deep level she needs from him, and it was almost a relief when he was offered a two-month photographic assignment in Scotland to record the effects of climate change on rivers and wildlife. It worries her how strongly her resentment resonated in her feelings for Giles; how she wanted to shout: 'But it's not your inheritance. It's mine and Bea and Will's.' These reactions shocked her and at one point she confided in Will while they were walking at Start Point. Standing high on the cliffs one wild and elemental morning she told Will what she was feeling and how ashamed she was. Will simply put an arm around her and hugged her closely to his side.

'Of course you feel like that,' he said, as if he were surprised that she should be upset. 'It's your first real home since your family died; you've brought up your own family there. Twenty years is a long time. Of course you're angry. We all feel angry when we're helpless. When we have no power we are unable to use our instinctive reactions to fight back, change things, and it can make us resentful, depressed, frightened. Acceptance is the hardest thing. But we can't change the way the sea is encroaching on our coasts each year. We can see it happening, and Bea and Giles are wise to suggest that we jump before we're pushed. At least we have choices and shall all be together.'

She cried then, weeping like a child, pushing her face against his shoulder, while he continued to hold her, calmly but firmly. Presently he produced a hand-kerchief and she was able to take deep breaths and steady herself.

'Sorry,' she muttered. 'Sorry, Will.'

'What for?' he asked prosaically. 'For being human? We must bite the bullet, darling Tessa. I'll try if you will.'

She bent to pat Bodger, her field spaniel, who, sensing her distress, was whining a little, pushing at her knees with his head.

'OK,' she said. 'I'll try.'

Now, as she listens to Bea and Will driving away to Dartmouth, she decides that she will go for a walk.

This need to walk, to get up and go, also worries her. More and more, she feels as if she is running away from herself, escaping from her emotions, unable to be quiet and calm. Bodger is stretched out in the sunshine by the back door. She changes her shoes, slips on a gilet and takes his lead from the peg.

'Come on,' she says. 'Let's walk down the lane.'

Bodger scrambles up eagerly: he likes his walk in the lane, new scents to follow. They go out of the gate together. Tessa doesn't put him on the lead; very little traffic comes this way and it's generally a tractor so she can hear it well in advance. She breathes deeply, aware of campion in the ditch and a drift of bluebells. The hawthorn is blossoming, creamy white against the brilliance of the sky. Already she is beginning to feel at peace.

As the lane begins to descend towards the village, she sees a figure striding up the hill. It's Leo. Tessa raises a hand in greeting. She likes Leo, although she is very slightly wary of him. He has a disconcerting knack of seeing through any pretence, he is self-contained, but he has a sharp sense of humour and he is kind. He and Will play chess and it fascinates her to watch them play and how Leo is totally impervious to Will's attempts to distract him. She crossed the cove one afternoon to speak to Bea and, going into the house, could hear Will's voice. She glanced into the sitting-room and saw him and Leo sitting at the table, the chessboard between them. Leo was deliberating over his next move, taking his time, and Will had picked up a book and was reading aloud:

. . . He had softly and suddenly vanished away —
For the Snark *was* a Boojum, you see.

26

She drew back, wanting to laugh, and went into the kitchen.

'Why,' she asked Bea, 'is Will reading *The Hunting of the Snark* aloud while he's playing chess?'

Bea raised her eyebrows. 'Surely you know by now that Will uses any means to win? He's doing it to irritate and annoy but you can't distract Leo that easily.'

Remembering the scene, Tessa is smiling as she approaches Leo and he smiles back at her.

'I've just seen Bea,' he says, bending to stroke Bodger. 'Are you off to the beach? Would you like some coffee to help you on your way? I'm going to have some.'

'I'd love some,' she says, aware of the need for company, distraction; irritated by it but unable to combat it. 'Thank you. Though poor old Bodger might feel he's being short-changed.'

'Well, he can potter around in the garden. We'll leave the door open for him.'

Tessa pauses by the back door, noting all the signs of activity: a wheelbarrow loaded with logs, a trug full of tools, empty plant containers. She knows how much Leo loves his garden.

'I wish I had your knowledge of plants,' she says, following him into the kitchen. 'I'm sure we could do much more with our little bit of garden if we had more experience between us.'

He's pushing the kettle on to the Aga's hotplate, reaching for coffee from a cupboard and spooning it into a cafetiere. Tessa sits at the kitchen table watching him, aware that he's preoccupied, not quite focused on her. But the invisible cloak of distance that Leo wears makes it impossible to ask, as she might another old friend, if he's OK. Instead she casts around for a

27

different topic of conversation and when his phone pings, she notices that he takes it quickly from his pocket, reads the message almost anxiously, before putting the phone on the dresser and smiling at her apologetically.

'Sorry,' he says. 'Sorry about that.' Although he doesn't say why. 'What were you saying? Yes, gardening. Well, I'm always happy to help.'

Before she can answer, Bodger comes in from the garden, causing more distraction. Leo finds some dog biscuits, which he keeps for visits from his family's dogs, pours the coffee and sits down.

'I've always thought that there's quite a lot you could do with your garden,' he says, almost at random. 'I'd enjoy a new challenge. How about it?'

She raises her cup to him, aware of his strange mood. 'You're on. Here's to our very own *Love Your Garden* project.'

★ ★ ★

After Tessa and Bodger have gone, continuing their walk down to the sea, Leo takes his phone from the dresser and rereads the message. Minutes before he met Tessa in the lane, he'd gathered all his courage and retyped and sent his text to Alice. Now he stares at her reply.

Thank you, dear Lion. X

There's nothing else, no clue as to when she might come, and he feels frustrated, confused, but strangely excited. His relief that she is still out there somewhere is so great that he almost mistakes it for happiness. He doesn't know what to do, whether to text again, to press her for information, but as usual his natural caution prevents him.

Instead he thinks back to their younger days, when Alice first began to stay with them after her mother died. He remembers how pleased he was to have a companion of nearly his own age, this slightly younger girl-cousin who was always so ready to join in, so grateful to be a part of his family. She would have been nine or ten, his sisters already in their teens. At fifteen, Helen was already self-confident, inclined to be judgemental, critical of Alice's need to be accepted. Meg was gentler, kinder, but influenced by her older sister, both of them slightly irritated by their mother's injunctions that they must be nice to their poor little motherless cousin.

Leo had no problem with this instruction. He was very happy to have someone who was so ready to fall in with his plans, share his games, keep him company. Alice was undemanding, funny, generous, and he began to look forward to the summer holidays when she came to Long Orchard for a few weeks. Even as they grew older, the bond held and now, as he clears away the coffee things, Leo's mind reels back into the past, remembering those happy times: rowing about in the old dinghy, long hikes out to Start Point and over the cliffs, Dartmouth Regatta.

Out of nowhere comes another memory: the Summer Ball at Britannia Royal Naval College. Helen's boyfriend at the time was a midshipman and he invited Meg and Leo to the Ball. As usual, Alice was staying for her annual summer holiday and it was only natural that she should partner Leo. At fifteen she was so pretty. Even now he can remember how proud he was to accompany her, how adorable she looked in her ballgown. And because she was Alice, his little cousin, there was no stress or strain, as there might have been with a girl he didn't know very well and had to impress. What a starry night it was: the young men in their uniforms with their lovely partners, the music, the champagne, the Band of the Royal Marines playing on the Quarter Deck high above the river.

'Oh, Lion,' she said, clutching his arm, her eyes no less starry than the ones shining above them. 'It's like magic. I wish it would never end.'

Now, Leo stands holding the cafetiere, wondering how he could ever have allowed her to vanish away from him; how he could have let her down so completely. Quickly he sets down the cafetiere, picks up his phone and texts.

I am here. How soon can you come? X

Another thought occurs to him. His mother kept a photograph album, recording the special moments of their childhoods, and a sudden need to see it again, to revisit the past, takes him across the kitchen and into the study. The album is on the bottom shelf of one of the tall bookcases.

Crouching, he lifts it out and carries it to the desk. He turns over the pages, ignoring the photographs of himself and his sisters as babies and very small children, turning the thick pages until he finds the first one of Alice. Here she is, standing between Meg and Helen, beaming at the camera, hands clasped in delight. The photograph is black and white, slightly fuzzy, and he continues to turn the pages until he finds one of himself with Alice beside him, perched on the upturned dinghy on the beach. This one was taken a few years later, it is in colour, and Leo is surprised by how thick and blond his hair was, how carefree he looks.

He tries to remember that boy on the beach fifty years before: the taste of salt, the smell of tar, the cries of the gulls. He peers at Alice, her long plait of hair, her bony knees drawn up, balancing on the hull, and he is filled with nostalgia. Why did no one warn him to hold tightly to the things he loved, to cherish the people who were precious to him?

Yet, he reminds himself, he is still here in the house that he loves; he has his family. Nobody can hold on to the past, and those eggshells in the compost heap, the sharp pains of regret and guilt, are a natural part of life. He continues to turn the pages and is confronted unexpectedly by several photographs of that wedding weekend. Here is Helen, looking self-consciously bridal, posed and slightly smug. Meg and Alice, in their bridesmaids' dresses, stand together, two pretty girls playing their part. And here is a group photograph taken later, out in the garden: the guests enjoying themselves, not posed, some even unaware it is being taken.

Leo slips the photograph from its fastening and takes it to the window so as to see it more clearly. Helen is laughing, raising a glass of champagne, and George is leaning over her, tender, protective, the brand-new loving husband. At a little distance, beneath the thorn tree, Alice is watching them. Amongst the jollity and fun, her expression strikes a bleak note as she stares at the traditionally happy couple with their new lives before them. She looks lonely, almost desperate, and terribly young.

Nineteen, thinks Leo. She was barely nineteen.

He tries to remember what happened after the wedding, after Uncle Philip told him that Alice made her way back to London, that she'd gone on an art's course

31

exchange to Italy, later that she'd joined a commune. Everything was vague, and after a while Leo gave up trying to contact her. He wondered if that was how she wanted it and, knowing her secret, he was unsure how he should proceed. Uncle Philip married again; Helen had a baby and Meg got married. Everyone had grown up; people were busy with their own lives, and Alice simply vanished, apart from the occasional impromptu meeting with her father. Until now.

Again Leo is swamped with such an intense relief that it is almost like joy. Now he will see her again; he will make amends. They will walk together on the beach, on the cliffs . . .

He hears his phone ping and he drops the photograph on the desk and almost runs back into the kitchen. The text is from his daughter-in-law and it takes him several moments to cope with his disappointment. Bethany sends some family news and tells him to have fun with Em on Friday. Leo stares at the text, baffled, still mentally in a summer forty years past. Em? Who is Em? Then he remembers Bethany's London friend: the fair-haired girl who is staying in Dartmouth for a couple of weeks whilst she works on a play she's writing. For some reason he invited her to coffee, or probably even lunch, whilst the family were all here for the weekend.

Leo curses silently under his breath as he taps out a message: he won't know what to say to her or how to entertain her and he regrets the foolish good manners that put him in this awkward position. But he is very fond of his daughter-in-law and so he will be hospitable to her friend. He remembers that Em was amusing, very sweet with the grandchildren, and had expressed an interest in the planning of the

32

arboretum. It will be fine. She will be a distraction from his present obsession with Alice and it will earn him brownie points from Bethany.

He texts to say that he's looking forward to it, wondering if he should confirm the time but he doesn't have Em's number. He switches on Jazz FM — Miles Davis playing 'It Never Entered My Mind' — and, opening the diary he keeps on the dresser, he picks up a pencil and writes 'EM' across Friday morning.

4

There is nobody sitting at the table in the alcove this morning, and Em takes possession of it, setting up her laptop, opening her notebook. The staff are getting to know her now, and when one of the girls calls, 'Mocha?' to her from behind the bar, Em smiles and nods, feeling pleased to be recognized as a local rather than a visitor, enjoying their interest in her. She's hinted to them about the play she's writing and it's rather fun to pretend that she might be a dramatist, to allow them to wonder if she might be writing about them.

As she pays for her mocha and returns to her table, however, she's thinking more of yesterday and her morning with Leo at Long Orchard, and when she opens her laptop it is an email to Bethany that she is beginning to compose in her head.

As she set out from Dartmouth to drive to Torcross she felt slightly nervous, wondering how it would work without Bethany and the family to help things along, but the journey across the cliffs and along the road beside the sea blew her mind and totally distracted her. She slowed the car several times, gazing out at the dramatic sweep of the coast, smooth yellow beaches tucked in tight beneath the cliffs, the sea rumpled as an old petticoat, and was frustrated to think that she was unable to incorporate this splendour into her play. Nevertheless, she knew that it was important to notice everything and she remembered some words of Ruskin's that her tutor had quoted: 'Does a man die at your feet — your business is not to help him, but to note the colour of his lips.' It was slightly disconcerting for her to realize that it was probably exactly what she would do: she is by nature an observer.

Now, as she begins her email to Bethany, her morning with Leo is clearly before her as she types.

I have to admit, Bets, that I was a bit dithery when I set out to see Leo yesterday. After all, I hardly know him and I was desperately trying to think of things we might talk about. I mean, we're poles apart when you think about it. I know you told me he was a land manager working for big estates, and I've lived all my life in London, so I was trying to think of some common ground, apart from you, of course. The thing is, though, that drive across the cliffs totally blew me away and when I got to his house I was so full of it that it got us right through meeting, making coffee and drinking it. He seemed really pleased that I loved it all so much, although I could tell that he was very slightly taken aback by my enthusiasm. He's not one of your demonstrative types, is he, and I could tell that he was thinking that I was a bit OTT. Well, you know what I'm like. I need to make everything a bit of a drama, make 'em laugh, and all that stuff. But it got us off on the right foot and he said, in that case I'd probably enjoy a walk along the beach and round the Ley. Is that the right word for that big freshwater lake? I have to say, Leo's no slouch, is he? He absolutely strode along. I could hardly keep up. And he knew so much about it all, telling me what all the birds were, and that if the sea levels rose much higher and came right over the road then the Ley and everything could be destroyed by the salt water. It was like having a natural history lesson, but really interesting. Then we went for lunch in the pub — amazing fresh fish — and he was very sweet and old-fashioned and insisted on paying for me. He said it was quite right as he'd invited me to lunch and this was easier than cooking. I really like him, Bets. But I tell you something that was funny. He's like a teenager with his phone. Every time it beeped, which wasn't that often, to be fair, he had it out of his pocket, checking — although lots of older people are like that, I suppose. But it just seemed funny. He seemed very slightly on edge, just a tad preoccupied, and I wondered if there were some kind of family drama going on. But, anyway, I totally loved it. I couldn't really think of any way I could return his kindness, though, so I just said that if he ever wanted to see my funny flat he was very welcome and then I could take him to lunch at Bayards Cove. Actually he was quite interested in where my flat is, and surprised when I told him I could see a bit of the river but I didn't quite have the nerve to make a date. I wish I had now.

Em sits back and rereads what she's written. She wonders if she's sounding a bit too keen but, after all, it's not like Leo is Bethany's dad or anything. He and Bethany get on really well so Em can't really see any harm in letting her best friend know she likes him too. Em tests her feelings, thinking about Leo.

She really likes his passion for the earth, the wildlife, the sea. He really cares about the planet. After lunch, when they got back, he took her up to the arboretum and the wildflower meadow. Once again she was completely bowled over by the magic of the wild-flowers, the tapestry of colour, and he told her their names, how good they were for bees and insects, and laughed at her excitement and enthusiasm.

'I can see I've made a convert,' he said. 'I hope that when you get home to London you'll plant up some window boxes.'

When they got back to the house, she asked if she could use the loo before she set off to Dartmouth. He gave her directions but remained in the garden whilst she went into the house, through the kitchen and the room beyond to the hall and the downstairs lavatory. On her way back, she was struck by the number of books in what was clearly Leo's study. Three walls had bookcases and there were small piles of books on the floor.

Instinctively she hesitated beside the big oak desk with its modern monitor and keyboard. Several pack-ets of photographs lay on it, the old-fashioned sort that you would have had to get printed and processed from Boots. It was wrong to pry but that line of Rus-kin's, 'Does a man die at your feet . . . ', was in her mind, and she leaned to look at the photographs, which spilled from the paper folders. Family groups, two girls and a boy, which she guessed were Leo and his sisters, and the same boy with a slightly younger girl. As she bent closer she heard a footstep in the room beyond and quickly she passed on through, coming into the kitchen and smiling at Leo, who was just entering through the door opposite.

Drinking her mocha, Em remembers how she smiled at him, made a joke about getting lost, and made her farewells. Now she sets down her cup and continues her email.

And the house is, like, wow, Bets. All those beams and the way the rooms all lead through to other rooms. You are so lucky to have this to come back to when you get fed up with city life. Leo's place and this little flat when your mum and dad don't want it — some people just get all the luck. Perhaps I might just cosy up to Leo and see if he'd like a younger wife. D'you think James would like me for a stepmum? Don't worry! Just kidding! Anyway, I need to do some work. Love to you all. Em xxxx

She sends the email, drinks some more mocha and opens her work file. There is a pitifully small amount of writing and she stares around her, hoping for inspiration, wondering how to make the connections she needs for the play. For instance, how could there be a connection with the elderly man reading his newspaper, the group of young mothers with their children sitting at the table in the window, and the attractive woman in the corner, staring into space as she sips her coffee? What are their stories; how could she use them? Em shakes her head in despair and decides to write a description of the café to get her started.

★   ★   ★

Tessa sips her coffee, watching the baristas behind the bar, listening to the background jazz music, but all her thoughts are inward. This dash to Dartmouth this morning was just another flight from this restlessness she's feeling, the loneliness and the awful sense of pointlessness. She thinks that she should get a job, but a career as a house and dog-sitter followed by twenty years of bringing up children doesn't really qualify her for much. She's had a few random part-time jobs during those years but not much to recommend her.

She's been envying the woman in the alcove, typing away like mad on her laptop. She looks very professional and Tessa wonders what kind of work she's doing. It must be nice to have the kind of job that you can do whilst sitting in Bayards Cove Café, drinking coffee.

The door opens and a tall, fair-haired man comes in. There are a few customers clustered at the bar, waiting to order, and the newcomer looks around for an empty table. As his glance sweeps Tessa, it stops and he does an almost ludicrous double-take. She, too, is staring at him, and he begins to smile and then comes towards her. Tessa is already rising to her feet, as if he is drawing her upwards, and when he holds out his arms to hug her and says, 'Hello, kiddo,' the years drop away and suddenly she is shot through with happiness.

'Sebastian,' she says, still hardly believing it. 'This is amazing. What are you doing here?'

He lets her go and sits down opposite her as she subsides back into her chair.

'My oldest boy is at the College. He's passed the Admiralty Interview Board and he's following his old dad into the navy. He's got a forty-eight-hour pass and I'm picking him up later. How about you?' His gaze flicks over her again and he smiles. 'You're looking pretty good.'

Foolishly, crazily, just for a moment, she is bereft of words. The sight of him, his presence, has robbed her of her common sense.

'This is so amazing,' she says again.

'Just don't start asking how many years it is,' he says. 'So dispiriting. Let's just agree it's a long time and leave it at that. I expect my dear sister told you that I'm divorced. I know you and she have never had secrets from each other.'

Tessa remembers hearing the news from Rachel round about the time when they were leaving the cove and everything was in chaos, and she nods.

'Yes, Rachel told me. I'm sorry about that, Seb. She said you'd been posted to Washington.'

He nods. 'I was but I'm back now at the MOD. Life's rich pageant and all that. So how are you? And Giles? Rather lucky bumping into you like this. Shall I order some coffee and do some catching up?'

'Yes,' she says, 'and it's as if she's coming back to life again, and it's painful and wonderful — and dangerous.

★   ★   ★

Em sits back, eases her shoulders and looks around her. She's written quite a nice little word picture of the café's interior and now she's wondering if she should have tried something more ambitious than a radio play. Perhaps it was foolish to imagine a world within a café; a scenario where people were interconnecting. The young mothers are still sitting at the table in the window, the elderly man is doing the crossword, the attractive woman in the corner has been joined by a man who is making her laugh. Watching them, Em decides that they aren't married, or long-term partners: they have too much to say to each other. They are engaged mentally, enjoying being with each other. When his coffee arrives, the man notices that his companion has already finished hers so he gets up to order another one for her.

40

Em sees that the woman quickly opens her bag, applies some lip gloss, flicks her short blonde hair. The man is flirting very slightly with one of the girls at the bar, who is laughing at something he's said, and when he turns back to the table he is still smiling. He's tall, good-looking, smartly dressed, probably nearer fifty than forty. The woman looks younger and as she looks up at him Em sees that indefinable look in her eyes, the sparkle that is impossible to hide. 'Love and a cough cannot be hid.' Em feels an odd need to call out a warning and mentally gives herself a shake. This is no business of hers, though it might be useful to her play. She will watch them for a while, make notes. She orders another mocha and settles down to observe. Ruskin would be proud of her.

5

Leo glances at his watch. In half an hour Helen and George will be arriving. Even as he mentally checks that he's made all the preparations, he's wondering how he will manage to cope if Alice should suddenly text to tell him she's on her way. The timing couldn't be worse. Although he rings her phone there is never an answer, not even an invitation to leave a voicemail, and he feels frustrated.

Since he's been living at Long Orchard — and especially since Jenny moved back to London — his sisters have considered it their right to continue to use the house for weekend breaks and occasionally for longer holidays in the summer. After his father died, Leo bought them out but on terms that make it impossible to refuse either Helen or Meg when they ask to come to refresh their spirits or seek a change of scene. And now that he's retired it's very difficult to think of a good excuse to deny them, unless his own family is staying.

Leo glances at his watch again as he paces up and down, through to the study, back into the hall. He wonders if he should tell them that Alice has been in touch, how he would phrase it, and immediately all the complications come flooding in. Supposing she had George's child all those years ago and is planning to bring him or her with her? Supposing it's a son who looks like George? The child would now be forty-four and Leo tries to imagine a scene in which Helen and George are confronted with his son or daughter. It occurs to him that he's never doubted that Alice spoke the truth; her horror was palpable. She and George were good friends — George's father and Uncle Philip served together in the army — and George's five years' seniority would have lent a glamour to his already sexy charm. Even Helen had felt the force of it and plunged into a whirlwind engagement and marriage, swept off her sensible feet.

Leo knows that Alice never wanted George to marry her. Nevertheless, that wedding day must have been so difficult for her — as it would be now for all of them if Alice were to confront George with a child at this late date. As usual, as they did all those years ago, Leo's anxieties for his sister crowd to the forefront of his mind. Loyal, sensible Helen doesn't deserve this. He guesses that life with George hasn't been all roses and it would be terrible after so long to confront her with her husband's love-child. He wishes now that he hadn't sent the texts to Alice urging her to come; she might just take him at his word. The old Alice was quite capable of simply turning up unannounced: the free spirit, here today and gone tomorrow.

He hears the sound of a car's engine, a door slamming and Helen's voice, and hurries out to greet them. Helen is directing the unloading of luggage whilst helping their elderly black Lab to jump down from the back of the car. When George retired they gave a home to this benign, gentlemanly fellow whose owner had died. Bax — named for some reason after the composer Sir Arnold Bax — has proved a very positive addition to their lives and everyone adores him. He follows Helen into the house, tail wagging, sure of his welcome. Leo has already got his special rug waiting for him by the Aga, and a few treats, which he gives to Bax whilst Helen looks around her in that familiar, assessing way to check that all is as it should be.

She gives her brother a hug, looks at him critically and then nods at him.

'You're looking well,' she says, and he feels as if he has passed some crucial test.

'You, too,' he says, smiling at her.

Helen never seems to change. Her short hair, thick and fair like his, has faded a little, but she has a lively look. George, following her in with the bags, has put on some weight but he still has a twinkle in his brown eyes and his dark hair is only lightly streaked with grey.

'How are you, Leo?' he asks, putting a bag down so as to give his brother-in-law a one-arm hug. 'This is kind of you. Lovely to get away for a few days.'

Leo returns his greeting, wondering why it feels as if everything has changed, as if he has a secret he must hide. After all, he's known Alice's secret for as long as Helen and George have been married.

'Can you manage those?' he asks, to hide this confusion. 'You're in your usual room. Tea? Coffee? Or is it wine o'clock?'

'Oh, I think so,' says Helen at once. 'We had a couple of tea breaks on the way down. A glass of wine would be very nice, Leo. We'll just take these up. Come on, George.'

George gives him a little wink and follows her out. There has always been this sense of conspiracy between him and George: an acknowledgement of Helen's bossiness whilst appreciating her excellent qualities. But today Leo's finding it hard. It's as if he can hear Alice's voice in his ear, senses her ghost at his elbow, and those eggshells pierce his heart. Bax sits watching him, hopeful but restrained, and Leo reaches for a few more treats.

'There you are, Sir Arnold,' he murmurs. 'Good fellow.'

Bax beats his tail appreciatively whilst Leo lines up some glasses and pours some wine. Helen and George reappear and he holds up the bottle.

'A rather nice Shiraz,' he says. 'I hope you approve. I'm wondering if you'd like it in the garden?'

'Too chilly,' says Helen. 'Or it will be soon. Still a bit early for that.'

And once again the ghost of Alice is at his elbow, murmuring in his ear, 'Helen has such a big pair of common-sense scissors. Always cutting things down to size.'

He remembers how he gave a little explosive snort of laughter before giving her a reproving nudge. Now, he smiles and nods.

'I'm sure you're right. Well, tell me all the news. The children and the children's children.'

His phone is in his pocket — he doesn't want a message popping up that anyone might read — and he's been in two minds whether to switch it off. It's crazy to be feeling like this, as if he's sixteen rather than sixty-four, but he wants to be ready to respond. In the end he's decided to turn off the bell but to leave the phone switched on so that he can do a check from time to time. He realizes that he's not concentrating, that Helen has that old familiar, quizzing look, and he steps quickly into the breach with a question about the newest grandchild so that any suspicions are deflected.

It's Helen who spots the photograph album the next morning. Beady-eyed Helen, who sees it only partially hidden on Leo's desk as she passes through the study and carries it triumphantly into the kitchen where George and Leo are having breakfast.

'I haven't seen this for years,' she says, sitting down and putting it on the table. 'Were you having a blast from the past, old Lion? Recapturing your youth?'

She begins to turn the pages, exclaiming as she recognizes the memories, and Leo curses silently, furious that he hasn't put the album back on the shelf. George grins at him.

'So embarrassing,' he murmurs, 'seeing ourselves in shorts, and our improbable haircuts.'

'Nonsense,' says Helen indignantly. 'He looks rather sweet. Oh, do look at us all down on the beach. And here's Mags on that pony she loved so much. What was it called?' She peers closer to see the faded words written below. 'Mags on Fudge'. Yes, I remember now. And here's you, Leo, on your first bike.'

Leo closes his eyes briefly and George gives a snort of amusement.

'Would you like some fruit salad,' he asks her, 'or some toast?'

But Helen is still turning the pages with delight. 'Here we are again,' she says, 'up on the moor having a picnic. And who's this with us? Oh goodness, it's Alice. What a funny little thing she was, so thin and waif-like. So sad that we all lost touch.'

Leo feels an odd contraction of his stomach but says nothing.

'It's so odd to see these black-and-white ones,'

Helen says, 'but of course that's all there was back then. Nineteen sixty-five. I was fourteen. Oh, now this is more like it. Here we are dressed to go to the Dartmouth Ball. Here's Alice again. She looks so sweet, and you in your black tie, Leo. Oh, do look, George.' She pushes the album towards him, smiling at Leo. 'So why did you get it out after all these years?'

This is so like Helen, never letting anything rest, ferreting things out, and Leo cannot think of any good answer.

'Perhaps he was doing a Proust,' murmurs George. 'You know, searching for times past, and all that. Could I ask if there's any more coffee, Leo?'

'Yes, of course.' Leo gets to his feet, grateful for the distraction and an unworthy surprise that his brother-in-law has even heard of Proust. Leo's glad that he's taken the photograph of the wedding group in the garden out of the book, but now he's wondering where he put it. He longs to check his phone and, for the first time, feels a sneaking sympathy with his teenage grandsons.

Bax comes in from the garden, thrusting his nose under Helen's arm, tail wagging. It's rained in the night and his paws and coat are wet, and she gives an exclamation of irritation, getting up to find a towel to dry his feet. Leo takes the opportunity to remove the album and pour coffee for them all.

'So what's the plan?' he asks. He knows that Helen always has a plan.

★　★　★

Helen isn't thinking about plans — she's thinking about Alice. As she dries Bax's paws she's remembering

47

how, back then, her small cousin always engendered such a negative reaction, and even now the photographs set off the same response. Was it her slender attractiveness, so much in contrast with Helen's own rather solid, blonde prettiness? She was always 'showing off': Helen's private description of the way Alice would suddenly dance for pure joy, pirouetting, flinging up her thin arms, or exclaiming in delight over small things: flowers, puppies, cake. Even as she grew older she was much too extravagant in her behaviour, and Helen was often embarrassed by Alice's affectionate hugs and gratitude. George always took her part, of course, but then he'd known her for ever. Uncle Philip and George's father were in the same regiment, so it was natural that George should look upon her as a part of the family: a little sister, almost.

Though there was a time, remembers Helen as she puts the damp towel on the Aga rail to dry, when she'd had a dreadful suspicion that it was more than that. It was at a party in London, there was a bit of a disco going on, and coming back from the loo, she glimpsed George and Alice dancing together. The memory is startlingly clear, even the music: Donna Summer's 'Love To Love You Baby'. Alice was wearing a long silky dress of a strange sea-green colour that complemented her brown-gold hair, which was falling down her back. In that brief moment Helen saw George pull Alice towards him, his hand hidden in her hair on her bare back, and she put both arms round his neck, holding him tightly. It was a typically extravagant Alice-type gesture yet Helen was pierced with a terrible and unexpected jealousy. Their embrace was so shocking in its intimacy. The crowds of dancers hid them from her sight, and when she next saw them

48

they were dancing apart, casual again. As the music finished, Alice simply turned away and George looked around as if seeking Helen and the friends they were with. They were not long engaged and Helen had no intention of showing any kind of weakness or insecurity, but later, unable to dismiss that little stab of jealousy, she charged him with it.

'You and Alice seemed to be enjoying a smooch earlier.'

He looked at her with his familiar jokey expression, half guilty, half laughing, always ready to disarm any attack, but seeing that this time she was not amused, he simply looked puzzled.

'Did we? Me and Al?' He shrugged and shook his head. 'She's a bit tense this evening, haven't you noticed? One of our friends has been seriously injured in an IRA bomb blast in Belfast. You know Al. Sensitive little soul, especially after a few drinks.'

As she turns back to the kitchen table, Helen remembers her response: an odd mix of relief at his casual dismissiveness, resentment that everyone always had to consider Alice's sensitivity, her motherlessness, even guilt about the dead soldier. Now, with an effort, she gets a grip on her emotions, sits down again at the breakfast table and begins to outline her plans for the morning.

★ ★ ★

George isn't listening to Helen's plans: he's turning the pages of the album, remembering Alice. He can't imagine Alice grown old. She's always caught like a fly in the amber of their youth: vulnerable, sensitive, graceful. The five years between them made any real friendship difficult as they were growing up. She was like a little sister, but her fragile beauty touched him.

'She needs affection,' his mother would say. 'She's missing her mother. What a tragedy it is.'

But when she was older, Alice had so many friends. She was always being invited to stay with them, to go abroad on holiday, to the theatre. Whilst he was learning the ropes at the investment bank in the City after university, she left school and began on a series of adventures. She worked in a gallery, at festivals, as a chalet girl.

'But what are you going to *do*?' he asked. 'As a serious job, I mean.'

'Why do I have to have a serious job?' she responded, laughing at him. 'Why can't I just be happy?'

He knew that she would consider all his answers to be stuffy, so he just shook his head. 'You're hopeless.'

She looked suddenly sad. 'I know,' she answered. 'But I can't help myself, Georgie.'

The childish use of his name disarmed him, her expression moved him, and he opened his arms to give her the usual affectionate hug. How often that had happened — and once, just once, it had been more than just a brotherly embrace. Much, much more.

'What's it like, Georgie?' she asked him. 'Being in love? Is it amazing?'

They'd been in his little flat after a small get-together for his flatmate's birthday. He and some friends had gone on to a club and George was going to drop Alice home before joining them. A few months earlier he and Helen had become engaged and the wedding was being planned. To be truthful, he was feeling the least bit nervous at the finality of his single

50

state and of the speed with which things were being planned.

'We might just as well get on with it,' Helen said, in her usual positive way, which he was already beginning to regard as bossy, but he could think of no good reason for slowing things down.

Alice was pulling on her coat and George reached out to help her. They stood together in the small hallway and she glanced round and up at him as he put it around her shoulders. He stared down at her, into those amazing eyes, and was suddenly filled with a sense of loss: of youth, of freedom, of choice.

'Not so's you'd notice,' he mumbled. 'Oh, Al. What am I doing?'

She turned within his arms, full of anxiety and compassion, and affection for him. She began to speak but he was already kissing her, and she was responding, hugging him close.

'Your coffee's cold,' says Helen.

She's staring at him suspiciously, as if she knows exactly what he's been thinking, and he puts the album aside, picks up his cup quickly, smiling, back in the present.

★ ★ ★

Watching them, Leo is aware of a change of atmosphere around the table. Helen and George seem oddly preoccupied and there is a current of hostility. His instinct tells him that this has been triggered by the photograph album and as he gets up, he casually takes it away with his plate and his coffee mug. He drops it on to the dresser and half conceals it with some letters and a book. How strange it is that Alice

51

is able to have this effect after so much time. He takes the opportunity to glance at his phone but there is no message.

He wonders how they would react if he were to say casually, 'Actually, I've had a letter from Alice. She's asked if she can come home.'

He can imagine the startled reactions, but would they be delighted, speculative, ready to welcome the prodigal? Until he knows more he's in no position to set the cat amongst the pigeons. He's frustrated, feeling helpless in his inability to move things forward, but he can only wait — and hope that Alice doesn't suddenly appear whilst Helen and George are here.

'Are you OK?' George asks quietly.

He's helping to clear the table and pauses beside Leo. His look is quizzical, as if he suspects that Leo is concealing something, and, just for a moment, Leo wishes that he could talk to his brother-in-law, tell him what's going on, ask him what really happened back then. He is certain that George has no idea that Alice was pregnant with his child, that he would be shocked, and even more worried that Helen should discover it, even at this late date. Leo can't begin to imagine what such a disclosure would have on their relationship. George is still watching him and he feels a little pang of anxiety. He's not used to dissembling.

'I'm fine,' he answers rather randomly. 'It's been a bit hectic these last couple of weeks. The kids have been down and one of Bethany's friends is staying at their flat in Dartmouth. A girl called Em. I've been detailed off to keep a fatherly eye on her.'

George quirks an eyebrow. 'Sounds interesting. Are we allowed to meet her?'

'Meet who?' asks Helen from behind them. And

Leo curses silently under his breath.

'I was just telling George that one of Bethany's friends is staying at their flat. She's on some kind of sabbatical from her advertising agency and she came over to see them when they were down last week.'

'Well, I was saying that we want to go into Dartmouth,' says Helen at once. 'Have you got her number? We could meet her for coffee or something. She might be a bit lonely if she's there on her own.'

'Yes,' answers Leo inadequately. 'Yes, I suppose we could.'

'Or you could invite her over for lunch tomorrow?'

'No,' he says quickly. 'No, coffee in Dartmouth would be good. I'll send her a text and see if she's free.'

George grins at him, gives him a little wink. 'Sounds like a plan.'

6

Tessa walks beside the sea, Bodger hurrying ahead, his paws sending up small spurts of sand. She hopes that he won't take a sudden plunge into the water; she doesn't want a very wet dog in the car, although she doesn't really mind, not at the moment, not in this strange mood that she's been in ever since she met Sebastian so unexpectedly in the café yesterday. How odd it is, this feeling of exultation, of excitement. How good it was to see him again after all this time, to hear him call her 'kiddo', to have the day-to-day routine suddenly overturned.

She plunges her hands into the pockets of her gilet and gazes up at the blue sky streaked with high cirrus, at the vapour trail of a plane blown into strange patterns, and she wants to laugh, to sing, to be silly. Bodger comes bounding back with a piece of driftwood in his mouth and drops it at her feet. She picks it up and looks at it: bleached-white wood, twisted and smoothed by the sea. He stares up at her expectantly and quickly she tosses it way up the beach and he goes scrambling after it, tail waving. She follows him, climbing higher up the shore, towards the shingle where the thrift grows, her thoughts still full of that meeting.

'We must stay in touch,' Sebastian said casually. 'I've probably got your phone number somewhere . . .'

She knew that he hadn't and said swiftly, 'Probably not the new one. Not since we moved.'

But both of them knew that neither was thinking

of a landline: not really. He was taking out his phone.

'Tell you what,' he said, 'if you give me your number I'll text you and then you'll have mine.'

'Great,' she said, taking her own phone out of her bag. 'I know it's crazy but I can never remember it so I have to look myself up.'

He watched her, smiling as she checked her contacts list and then read the number to him. He typed it in and put the phone back in his pocket, still smiling, and she thought that it was so like him not to do it at once but to take his time. When they left the café they walked together across the town towards the Embankment where she'd parked the car.

'That was fun,' he said, holding the door open as she climbed in. 'Perhaps we could do it again sometime?'

'That would be good,' she said. She hesitated. She'd already told him that Giles was away and she didn't want to look too keen. 'I'll text you,' she said, and he grinned down at her as she shut the car door.

She was barely out of the town, driving through Warfleet, when her phone beeped. Glancing in her mirror, she quickly pulled over to one side. There it was:

Would Monday morning be too soon? I've got to drop Nick off. Seb

She remembered that he was taking his oldest boy out from the College on a forty-eight-hour pass and she decided she'd go with it.

Great. Same time. Same place. T x

She hesitated over the kiss but put it anyway. She and Sebastian went back a long way, his sister was her oldest friend. No harm in a kiss.

Now, standing on the beach, listening to the tide,

Tessa gives a little shiver. No harm in a kiss. She remembers how they'd made love, all those years ago, how much she'd loved him with a young girl's romantic passion, and once again she's filled with an overwhelming sense of excitement and happiness.

'It's crazy,' she says aloud, to the sea and the gulls, and she knows it's foolish — and dangerous — but the prospect of seeing him again on Monday pushes common sense into oblivion. He was her first lover, though she knew quite well she wasn't his. And then later it happened again, they got engaged — and then Tessa met Giles and suddenly she'd seen her feelings for Sebastian in a different light: an infatuation, a need to be loved after the death of her family, gratitude for his kindness.

Standing here on the beach, it's necessary that she should remind herself of this: that her infatuation for Sebastian had been just that, an infatuation, and that they'd parted with relief on both sides. Talking to him again, laughing with him, it's clear to remember why she'd imagined herself in love with him. He's so easy to be with, and more than twenty years on he's still very attractive. He's made her feel alive again after these last months of depression, of leaving the cove, of not feeling totally in tune with Giles. And after all, what harm can there be in renewing this friendship? Even as she asks herself the question she knows that she is being naïve. There is always danger in a discontented woman and a divorced man resuming an old, loving relationship. Yet Tessa can't bear the thought of not seeing him again. Already he's brought colour and fun back into her life. Even with Will and Bea at hand she's lonely: missing Charlotte and Henry, missing the solace and beauty of the cove, and missing Giles, away again on another project. Their lives have always been slightly semi-detached because of his work but it hasn't mattered until now. Now, there is no hurly-burly of family life to make this new house a real home, and it is as if she is reliving the loneliness of those awful days when her parents and her brother died. It's no wonder that now, as then, she should be glad to see this old friend whose family gave her so much love and support. Why shouldn't she see him again?

As if in answer to her question, her phone beeps. Taking it out, she reads the message.

Could we make it a bit earlier on Monday? Would 10.00 be too early?

For a moment she hesitates, conflicted with a confusion of emotions: loyalty, need, self-justification. Then she texts one word:

Great.

Bodger is back with his piece of driftwood. She takes it and throws it in the direction of the car park, and follows him back to the car. As she gets in and switches on the engine she suddenly remembers that Bea and Will have invited her to lunch. Glancing at the car clock, she gives a little gasp of dismay. She must hurry, or she'll be late.

★   ★   ★

'No sign of the car yet?' Bea is asking Will, peering from the window.

'Not yet,' answers Will placidly. 'But there's no great rush. Only soup and cheese, after all. Nothing to get anxious about.'

The trouble is that dear old Bea is a stickler for

timing. Everything is prepared, and she'll be on edge now until Tessa arrives. Even as Bea stirs the soup again, glancing at her watch, Will hears the car's wheels on the gravel and a door slam.

'There she is,' he says with relief. 'Perfect timing.'

He gets to his feet and opens the door so as to welcome Tessa whilst Bea takes the warmed rolls from the oven.

Tessa appears all in a rush. 'Sorry. I was down on the beach with Bodger and lost track of the time. I've left him next door in the kitchen.'

She gives Will a hug, and he senses some kind of excitement emanating from her. Perhaps Giles is dashing home for a few days, or one of the children.

'Everyone OK?' he asks casually, as she comes into the room, which is both kitchen and dining-room.

'As far as I know,' she answers. 'Gosh, that smells good.'

Will sees her glance around and he recognizes the slight drop in her mood, the change of expression on her face, and he knows what she's thinking. She's comparing this smart, modern kitchen, with its dining area and double-glazed windows, to the old house in the cove. Tessa is regretting the absence of the character, the views and the continuous sea-music. She is unable, or unwilling, to appreciate the advantages this new home has to offer them. It seems impossible for her to be positive about them.

It's bad timing, thinks Will, that both of her children should now be away at university before they were able to make their mark on the new house — to transform the place into something familiar. Bea has seized on the good points; is quick to point out the conveniences, and he can see them, too. But he and

Bea are old. As he watches Tessa helping Bea, he is glad to see that the slight drop in her spirits has passed and the earlier febrile excitement has returned. It's in the slight curl of her lips and the glint in her eye. He wonders if she is planning some kind of surprise and feels pleased that there is something of the old Tessa in that look after these months of difficulty. All will be well.

★ ★ ★

Bea, too, has noticed Tessa's sparkle but is slightly suspicious of it. It has the quality of mischief rather than simple cheerfulness. At the same time it's good to see her looking so alive: so much more like the old Tessa. She's telling them about an interview she's been to, making Will laugh; suggesting that she might become a dog walker again.

'After all,' she says, helping herself to a roll, 'with everybody working these days I'd be in huge demand.'

'All very well on a day like today,' observes Will, 'but think of the winter, the rain and the gales. And Bodger would hate it.'

Tessa laughs. 'Well, thanks for your positive reaction. I'd better consider plan B. Oh, blast. I haven't got a plan B.'

Will laughs with her and Bea joins in with this jollity, though she suspects these high spirits and she tries not to show it. It's good to see Will enjoying himself, to have him walking again, after the operation — though she lives in terror of him having a fall. He teases her, tells her that she's an old fuss-pot, but she knows that they are both aware of how lucky they are to have each other: the shared love and support and companionship. She experiences the familiar churning of fear in her gut whenever she imagines life without Will, and she gets up to clear away the plates lest the others should notice her change of mood.

'Well, she was looking very chipper,' says Will, when Tessa has gone. 'It's good to see her so much more like the old Tessa.'

'It is,' agrees Bea, 'but I can't help wondering what brought on the sudden change.'

'I thought that, too,' says Will, beginning to load the dishwasher. 'I wondered if Giles might be coming down for a quick break but she didn't mention it. Perhaps she's just beginning to accept the changes.'

Bea raises her eyebrows. 'It seems a rather sudden transformation. And also rather more than a simple coming to terms with life. She's a bit like a child who's going to a party.'

'I know.' Will straightens up and turns round to look at her. 'Perhaps she's got a surprise in store, planning a treat.'

'But for whom?'

He laughs. 'You've got your matron face on. 'Tears before bedtime!' So the girl's happy. Let's all enjoy it. I'm going to read the paper.'

This is synonymous with 'I'm going to have a snooze' and Bea nods. Perhaps Will is right and there's a simple reason for Tessa's high spirits. Yet at the back of her mind she seems to recognize the symptoms: the flushed cheeks, the sparkling eyes, the laughter.

She looks like a girl in love, thinks Bea, and remembers how once she'd been in that crazy, foolish state in her unreciprocated infatuation for the married History Master, Tony Priest, back in that little prep school on the edge of the New Forest. Even now, she still feels humiliated by her feelings for him: how a simple greeting from him, a smile, could almost overwhelm her.

Love makes fools of us all, she thinks, but not Tessa, surely? How can it? She loves Giles and her children.

Bea goes out through the utility-room and into the small courtyard, which Will has been making into a cheerful sitting-out place with pots and planters, and a pretty tree in a large tub to lend some shade. It's warm and sheltered here, and Bea sits down on the wooden bench and raises her face, eyes closed, to the sun. It is necessary to be calm and rational; there is no reason to feel absurdly anxious simply because Tessa suddenly looks so oddly happy. There has been nothing lately in her behaviour, in her routine, to indicate that anything has altered. Nevertheless, Bea's instinct warns her that there has been a change and that, in some way, Tessa is vulnerable. Bea knows that Tessa is lonely, unsettled. But how to protect her? How to arm her against danger?

Sitting in the warm sunshine she begins to drowse. She is travelling back in time, remembering times past . . .

Sunday morning. The chapel was full but the faint warmth from the heaters had not yet dispelled the chill of the frosty December morning. The boys' breath appeared in smoky puffs and they rubbed their hands together, blowing out their cheeks, exaggerating the cold. Ever vigilant from her vantage point at the back of the choir stalls, she watched the small boy opposite. His face was dreamy and peaceful as he unobtrusively slid his fingers under the thigh of his even smaller companion and pinched the bare flesh. The cry of anguish was frozen on his victim's lips as she leaned

61

forward to look sternly at both of them. They stared back at her with innocent, guileless expressions, but she saw the sharp jab of an elbow in retaliation and smiled to herself. The headmaster was reading the lesson for the First Sunday in Advent:

' ' . . . it is high time to awake out of sleep . . . The night is far spent, the day is at hand; let us therefore cast off the works of darkness, and let us put on the armour of light . . . ' '

She could see Tony Priest, his head bent, and she felt anxious, although she can't remember why . . .

A bee blunders past, almost brushing her cheek, and Bea shakes herself awake, surprised by the vividness of her dream, but her anxiety remains.

7

Em stands on the Embankment, looking upriver, watching one of the riverboats gracefully avoiding an outrigger as it heads towards its mooring. She loves to watch the river traffic, to hear the steam train hoot as it travels along the opposite bank, to watch the sailing-dinghies swooping across the path of the ferries. Early holidaymakers stroll along the Embankment, eating ice cream and warding off the importunate gulls. It's good to be a part of all this, to feel that she's not just a visitor but that she lives here, even if it's just for these few short weeks.

All the time now, though, some part of her mind is working on how this might become an actuality: how she might find some way of staying, of truly belonging. Since she's been here, living in this magical place and writing her play, she's begun to believe that she's stepped out of the ordinary world into a different dimension where unusual things happen. How strange it was, for instance, that Leo should suggest meeting with his sister and brother-in-law; to have coffee with them. Of course, she's his daughters-in-law best friend, but even so, Em is rather excited by the fact that Leo thought of it.

She knows it's crazy but she's beginning to feel definitely attracted to Leo, so much so that she couldn't resist emailing Bethany to tell her about this new invitation and speculating on the reason for it.

It's rather sweet of him, isn't it, Bets? I mean, he doesn't really know me but he obviously wanted me to meet them . . .

As she remembers the email, Em is suddenly driven by a need to see if Bethany has answered it. Turning away from the river, she crosses the road, making her way to Bayards Cove. It's still quite early, the church bells are ringing, and the café has not yet begun to be busy. She waves a greeting, smiles a 'Yes, please,' to the suggestion of a mocha and puts her bag on the table in the alcove. This table has become her territory and she feels quite upset if she finds it occupied.

Having paid for and collected her mocha, Em settles herself comfortably and opens her laptop. She looks at her emails, and here is one from Bethany. Smiling to herself she begins to read it.

All I can say, babe, is if Leo is interested in you then you'll be the first woman to achieve that since Jenny! But, seriously? I mean, come on. He's sixty-four! Old enough to be your dad! I know he's very attractive, sexy even, but it seems a bit weird, though that's probably because he's James's father.

But look, what do I know? It does seem odd that he should have brought Helen and George over for coffee, I'll admit that. (By the way, if we're doing the older man thing, what did you think of Gorgeous Georgeous???) I agree he didn't need to do that. To be honest, I've sometimes wondered if he might be gay, but actually he just seems to be one of those totally self-sufficient men who don't really need anyone else outside family and friends. But, like I say, what do I know?

I'm not saying anything to James about this, by the way, and as far as I'm concerned, babe, if you just turn out to be soulmates, well, great. But please think about that age gap, if not for now, for later. Anyway, what's the next move?

Em pushes her laptop back a little and reaches for her mocha. This isn't quite the reply she was hoping for. She's been imagining a bit more girly excitement, and the age reference, she thinks, is slightly overdone. Thinking that Leo might be gay comes as a shock — this has never occurred to her for a moment — but she doesn't take it seriously. Em thinks about him, remembering how he behaves, his humour and his charm. It was true that when he introduced her to his sister the emphasis was on Em being Bethany's friend, but then it would be, wouldn't it? Actually, Helen had rather reminded her of his wife, Jenny: slightly bossy, tending to take charge of them all. They'd met in the Royal Castle where a few people, both staff and customers, knew them and stopped for a chat. George flirted a little with the woman who brought their coffee, but then Em could imagine that this was simply his habit. He *was* rather gorgeous. Helen had questioned her closely about why she was in Dartmouth and about her work, and Leo came to her rescue, which was very sweet of him.

Em drinks her mocha, weaving Leo's every small gesture and word into a reason for believing that he's interested in her.

And, after all, if she is the first woman since Jenny to attract him then clearly he's going to be very cautious. She wonders how she might make the next move; to encourage him.

65

The elderly gentleman has arrived with his newspaper. He smiles at her as he sits down a few tables away.

'How's the *magnum opus* coming on?' he asks genially, and she smiles and then makes a face, pulling down the corners of her mouth, indicating that it's not going well.

'Muse deserted you?' he asks sympathetically. 'Perhaps you need something stronger than coffee.'

She laughs with him, feeling the warmth of his friendliness, happy to be here in her corner. But his question has made her feel guilty. It's several days now since she's done any work on her play and, putting down her cup, she pulls her laptop towards her and opens the file. As usual she's slightly shocked by the lack of content and decides that she really must concentrate, work harder. It's difficult to imagine any intrigue or secrecy going on amongst the clientele here, though it's such a perfect setting. She tries to picture what it's like in the winter with the woodburner alight, cosy against the gales blowing outside, and wonders whether she should make it a Christmas story. Idly she imagines herself still here in the winter, and her mind flips back to working out a scenario that might enable her to stay here. She begins to think of how she might contact Leo, how to find a reason to see him again. She remembers that she hasn't yet returned his lunch at the pub at Torcross, and she wonders how she could word an invitation that would sound perfectly friendly and natural. She racks her brains, trying to think of somewhere she would like to visit that he might enjoy showing her: somewhere she hasn't been yet.

As if on cue, the elderly man leans forward, attracting her attention.

'The place to go if you're stuck is Agatha Christie's home just up the river. Greenway. That should inspire you. Ever been there? Lovely spot. You'd enjoy it. You could get a river trip to it.'

Em stares at him. It seems so appropriate, so absolutely right, that she beams at him. She can already feel the text to Leo forming in her head. She raises her cup to her friendly neighbour.

'Thank you,' she says. 'That sounds amazing.'

★ ★ ★

But Leo is busy and doesn't see Em's text come in. Fearful lest Helen or George should somehow intercept a message from Alice, he switches his phone off and puts it in his desk in the study. They've all enjoyed a walk over the cliffs at Start Point and now Bax is asleep on his rug and Leo is preparing a light lunch for them before they go home.

Helen, though, will not let the past lie undisturbed. She's unearthed the photograph album again and is turning the pages, commenting on this photo and that, reminding Leo of happy times back in the day, and he is going along with it and hoping to avoid any awkward questions about Alice. George sits at the table reading the newspaper they picked up at Stokeley Farm Shop on the way home and is apparently preoccupied with the day's news. Though, in his heightened state of awareness, Leo suspects that he's protecting himself from any questions from his wife.

Certainly there's a purpose to Helen's busyness and Leo isn't really surprised when she says to George: 'Of course, you probably knew Alice better than we did, didn't you? After all, she introduced us.'

She slants the album towards him, indicating a photograph, but George seems reluctant to be distracted from his newspaper and Helen is obliged to repeat her question. He glances up at the photo, puzzled, indifferent.

'What?' he asks. 'Who? Oh, Alice. Yes, I suppose I knew her pretty well. But she spent a lot of time with you all, didn't she? She was your cousin, for heaven's sake. I only saw her spasmodically and there was quite a big age gap. Funny little girl, wasn't she?'

He returns to his reading and Leo watches Helen frown, her lips tighten a little, and he is filled with tension. How terrible it is to know someone else's secret. Again he wonders what would happen if a car should pull up in the driveway and Alice should get out. How could he explain to Helen and George that he had told her to come back; to come home?

As he prepares the lunch he knows that it is much too late to tell them that he and Alice have been in touch, and he just prays and hopes that he can get them on their way before his secret is out. But at the same time he knows that this isn't going to go away: that Alice might very well come to Long Orchard and that he will have to be open about it. It's simply that he needs to know more, to know whether Alice did in fact have George's child, and if she is now going to confront them with him — or her.

Every time Helen turns a page of the album, he tenses, waiting for another observation, until he is able to say: 'Right! Lunch is ready. Shall I take that, Helen, to give you a bit more room?'

And he whisks the album away, putting the dishes in front of her, offering her a glass of wine.

'None for George,' she says, sharply. 'He's driving.'

George makes a humorous, resigned face as he folds his paper.

'Story of my life,' he says. 'That looks good, Leo.'

He embarks on a story about one of the grandchildren, requesting embellishment from Helen, which she is very ready to provide, and Leo sits down with an inward sigh of relief and allows himself to relax.

After lunch, bags are brought down, the car loaded, Bax is encouraged to jump in. Never has Leo been so happy to say goodbye and wave them off, but he's realized that from now on he must be ready: he must let them all know that he has heard from Alice and that she might be making a visit to Long Orchard. His anxiety is about how to disseminate the news, and how to be ready for any revelations on Alice's part, but he simply can't imagine how he can do this without disclosing the secret that he and Alice share, and causing damage within the family.

Leo closes the gate behind the car, gives a final wave and goes back into the house and into his study. Opening the drawer of his desk he takes out his phone and checks the texts. There are several but none from Alice. This time he's relieved. Having longed to hear from her he has suddenly been shown how devastating a revenant might be.

But there is a text from Em. He reads it rather blankly. It seems that she is inviting him to accompany her to visit Greenway, Agatha Christie's home on the River Dart. He can think of no reason at all why he should want to do this but can't think of how to say so politely. Leo groans aloud. How complicated his life has become. He remembers a rhyme his mother used to say to them when they were children.

O what a tangled web we weave,
When first we practise to deceive!

But it wasn't my deception, he thinks crossly. It's not my web.

He pockets his phone and goes into the kitchen to clear up the lunch.

★   ★   ★

'Well, that was fun,' says George, as they drive away, through the village and on to Torcross Line. 'So which way? Five Mile Lane? Or the coast road?'

He's aware of a slightly placatory note in his voice, an attempt to wheedle Helen into a jollier frame of mind. Ever since she saw that wretched photograph album there's been a distinctly frosty air: an accusatory tinge to her demeanour, as if she's remembering the past — and not in a good way.

And after all, thinks George, we're talking more than forty years ago, for goodness' sake. And so what if Alice and I shared a little moment? I wasn't married, dammit.

He's aware that his guilt is making him feel the least bit defensive, perhaps even causing him to misjudge Helen, and he makes a greater effort to behave normally.

'We'll split the difference and cut up through Strete,' he says. 'It was good to get down before the Bank Holiday. The traffic shouldn't be too bad.'

He continues to talk at random whilst Helen stares ahead until she says: 'It's odd though, isn't it, the way Alice just disappeared like that?'

George's heart sinks but he's been preparing him-

70

self and he's able to answer quite nonchalantly.

'Not really,' he says. 'It's that sort of age, isn't it, when young people do cut loose and go off. Gap years, travelling, that sort of thing. Ours did it. It's not as if she was totally out of touch with her father. Did you actually think about it at the time? Did Mags or Leo?'

It's a while before Helen replies.

'No,' she says at last, reluctantly. 'Obviously we'd just got married and Mags was getting engaged . . . '

'Well then,' he says, just a shade too heartily. 'Knowing Alice, she probably joined a commune or something.'

'It was just seeing those photographs,' says Helen, and George curses silently under his breath. 'She always looked so, well, vulnerable.'

Suddenly, again, he remembers the way she looked up at him: 'What's it like, Georgie? Being in love? Is it amazing?'

His heart is pierced with a sharp pain of guilt and regret, and for a moment he cannot speak. Luckily Helen is too deeply immersed in her own thoughts to notice the sudden clench of his hands on the wheel, his change of expression, and he is able to pull himself together before she speaks again.

'She was a very needy child,' she observes, and the old Helen is more in evidence now. 'Always wanting shows of love, always very extravagant in her affection. Of course, the grown-ups were always ready to give her plenty of that.' She glances sideways at him: a considering, very slightly contemptuous look. 'I remember you were always ready do your share, too.'

George decides not to take the bait, to be defensive, but simply sighs.

'Give it a break, love,' he says wearily. 'How many

71

years are we talking here? Are we really having this conversation?'

To his relief, Helen shifts in her seat, stares back at the road. Alice's shade is still between them but for the moment Helen has decided on a stand-off.

★ ★ ★

Helen sits in silence, unaware of the beauty of the passing countryside. What power old photographs hold: an ability to touch the heart, to swing you back to a different world, to a time when you were young and hopeful; confident of the future, sure in your decisions and choices. She feels unsettled, melancholic, a strange sadness for those happy, smiling children who were so confident that life would be kind, fun, rewarding. Her parents looking so young and strong, ponies, dogs, all long gone. Yet her own life has been good despite having to keep an eye on George's predilection for pretty women, and the ups and downs of parenthood. So why should she feel the little nag of guilt when she saw those photos of Alice looking so waif-like, or remembered that sharp sting of jealousy when she saw George dancing with her little cousin, his hand sliding up her bare back under the thick, curling hair?

Forty years ago, she reminds herself. More than that. Get a grip.

And after all, it wasn't her job to keep track of her cousin; Alice's father would have been doing that and it was true that she was never in the same place for long. So why this strange sense of loss? Memories flitting in and out of her mind give her a feeling of insecurity, of being untethered. That child, wistful,

72

longing for love, has vanished, nobody knows where; she might even be dead.

'I suppose,' she says, uncertainly, 'that we could track her down somehow.'

George glances sideways at her, looking puzzled, even slightly alarmed. She shrugs, surprised at herself.

'She's family, after all,' she says, almost defensively.

She's aware that she's being irrational, having spoken rather derogatively of Alice, and of George's friendship with her, but she's struggling with this odd sense of guilt, of a kind of debt to the past. The photograph album has opened up old feelings, memories, and she can't just pretend it hasn't happened.

8

Sebastian arrives first in the cove. He pauses to glance into the café then walks out on to the quay to watch the Hauleys packed with cars executing their mid-river *pas de deux* as they pass and turn, heading for the ferry slipways. It's good to stand in the sunshine with no demands on his time, no responsibilities, just the pleasure of the prospect of this meeting with Tessa. He's enjoying being free.

'You should never have married,' his mother once said to him. 'Your heart was never in it.'

Perhaps he should have married Tessa. She was so sweet, so loving, that he'd persuaded himself that he loved her in return — and then she met Giles. To be honest it was rather a relief: his feelings for her were confused. His mother and sister had practically adopted her when her family were killed so disastrously and his own elder-brother protectiveness morphed into a kind of loving that was easily mistaken for the real thing — until she met Giles. There was no bitterness, no bad feeling, and how good to meet up with her again so unexpectedly . . .

And here she is, walking towards him, smiling, and quite instinctively he holds out his arms to her and they embrace, naturally and easily, old friends meeting up after a long separation.

They go into the café together, order coffee, choose a table. He notes that she decides to sit away from the windows and the door, well back in the café in a corner, but decides that there isn't necessarily an agenda.

She's already told him that Giles is away for a few weeks, that the children are at uni, so he feels quite at ease. Having spent most of the last conversation catching up he decides to move them back past their families and their work and commitments to the far past, which only the two of them share.

'So,' he begins, once the coffee has arrived, 'you're still doing the dog-walking. That's good. And I really want to meet Bodger. After I left last time I was trying to remember the names of some of those dogs. There were so many of them. Do you remember Romulus and Remus?'

Tessa begins to laugh and he watches her appreciatively. She still looks so young. So natural.

'Of course I do. It was the best job in the world. Lovely dogs living in beautiful places.'

They played the 'D'you remember game'?, happy together, at ease with one another, until he says, 'And what about that great bear of a dog you were looking after up near Mary Tavy? Huge animal with an extraordinary name. What was he called?'

Tessa's expression changes, softens.

'Charlie Custard,' she says. 'He was a Newfoundland. Oh, how I loved him.'

'That's right. Charlie Custard.'

And along with the name come other memories, of the night they shared together, and Sebastian suddenly feels almost nervous, as though he has gone too far. He looks at Tessa, searching for her reaction, and he knows that she is remembering, too. Charlie Custard's owner lived on the edge of Dartmoor, and Sebastian had telephoned Tessa from the dockyard, suggesting that he might take her out to supper if she could come and fetch him. He remembers how she

75

picked him up at the Camels Head Gate and he saw this enormous black dog watching him as he flung his grip on to the back seat. 'Good God,' he said. 'Do you know you have a bear in your car?'

Across the table Tessa is looking at him, her expression wary, and he shakes his head, smiling.

'Memories,' he says. 'Good ones.'

She smiles at him; the younger Tessa, vulnerable and sweet, and he feels the old desire to protect. He steers the conversation into less emotional channels, they agree to meet again at a place to be decided on, and they part. Tessa says she needs the loo, so he leaves first, striding away from Bayards, through the town towards the car park. But it's only when he's sitting in the car with the engine idling that Sebastian allows his memory full rein.

Staring through the windscreen at nothing in particular, he travels back in time to that odd little bungalow belonging to Charlie Custard's owner, and to that evening with Tessa. They went out for supper to the Elephant's Nest and then came back to sit together in front of the fire with Charlie Custard snoring heavily on the hearthrug. They'd made love and he stayed the night with her. He remembers how he had wakened in the night to find Tessa gone and, needing a cigarette, he slid out of bed. Picking up his trousers from a chair, his attention was caught by a movement outside and he paused, staring out of the window. Across the pale, moon-washed grass of the meadow, Tessa walked, slim and straight in her long dressing gown, the great dog at her heels. There was something almost medieval in the scene and he was moved beyond his usual desires and sensations. For the first time he saw Tessa as other men might see

76

her: not as the adoring girl who could be picked up and put down as his whim took him, but as an intelligent, successful and desirable young woman. As he stood watching her, he remembered the name she had mentioned earlier in the pub. 'Giles,' she'd said. 'Giles brought me here.'

Turning abruptly, he dragged on shirt and trousers, crammed his bare feet uncomfortably into his shoes and went out through the kitchen and into the garden. She turned as he came through the gate, standing still, her hand resting on the dog's head. She looked remote and unapproachable in the ghostly light and he knew a moment of fear. He came up to her, took her by the elbows and stared down into her face.

'I love you,' he said. 'I've just realized it. Will you marry me?'

There is a sharp tap on the car's window and Sebastian is suddenly aware that a woman is trying to attract his attention. He lowers the window and she smiles at him apologetically.

'Sorry,' she says. 'You looked miles away. Only we were wondering if you were leaving. The car park's full, you see . . .'

'Yes,' he says, 'yes, of course,' and he pulls out and drives away, feeling a fool.

★　★　★

Em is rather put out to see the blonde woman and her friend sitting at the alcove table when she arrives at the café. It's silly to feel so proprietorial but she can't help it. Instead she sits on the sofa in the bay window by the wood-burner and hopes that a different viewpoint might inspire her. The trouble is that she can't get

77

Leo out of her mind. She's becoming obsessed with him. All the time she's ordering her mocha, chatting to the girls behind the bar, setting up her laptop, she's thinking about his text and trying to put different, positive, connotations on it. It's difficult, however, to be upbeat about his simple response.

Thanks for this. My sister and brother-in-law are still here. Be in touch.

She stares again at the message, wondering how she can reply. It leaves very little room for further negotiation and she's feeling frustrated and disappointed. She stares around the café, raising a hand in response to the elderly man's cheerful wave, glancing again at the woman at the alcove table. Em is confirmed in her first instinct that those two aren't married. They have far too much to say to each other, they laugh too much for a couple who have been in a long relationship. She watches the woman's face, her eyes intent on her companion, and she sees a woman in love, oblivious of anyone but the man across the table.

Just for a moment, Em forgets about Leo and stares at her. 'Does a man die at your feet . . . ' She wonders how on earth she could describe that expression: tender, excited, vulnerable. It would certainly be impossible to transpose it into a radio play. Em feels inadequate, and her former restlessness and discontent regarding Leo's text returns.

It's like I'm in love with him, she thinks, but I'm not . . .

Instinctively her gaze returns to the couple in the alcove, their complete absorption in each other, and even as she watches they begin to get up, collecting belongings, preparatory to leaving. She sees the man lean forward and, holding the woman by the shoulders, kiss her on each cheek, and then quickly and lightly on the mouth. He turns and comes across the room, between the tables, and Em stares at him, noting his tall attractiveness, and his preoccupied expression. He sees nothing and nobody, and goes out into the May sunshine oblivious to anything around him. Em sees that the woman is staring after him, mechanically, picking up her bag, watching him leave, before heading into the back of the café to the lavatories.

When she comes out again, her face wears that similar inward-looking gaze of her companion, and as she passes, Em longs to grab her by the arm, to say: 'Wait. Talk to me. Tell me what you're thinking; what you're feeling. Explain it to me.'

She sips her mocha, wondering what the woman's reaction would be, and on an instinct opens her laptop.

Honestly, Bets, what is it when you're weirdly obsessed with someone? I know it's crazy but I can't get Leo out of my mind. It's like being in love, but it's not really. At least I don't think it is. Help me! And for God's sake don't you dare tell James. How terrible love is, isn't it? Destructive but life-affirming. Has he said anything to either of you? About me, I mean. No, of course he hasn't! Why would he? Sorry, I'm just being totally mad. It's this writing stuff getting to me. And don't do that counselling thing. Try to imagine that he isn't James's father and what you'd be saying to me.

Em sits staring at this for a moment, she rereads it and then without giving herself the chance to change her mind, she sends it. She opens her work file and tries to concentrate on her play.

79

When Tessa gets home she knows that she's in no fit state to talk to anyone. Her morning with Sebastian has completely disorientated her and she knows that it will be very difficult to dissemble under Bea's sharp gaze. She wishes now that she'd left Bodger on his own in her kitchen but Will, who was working in the garden when she was getting the car out, offered to have him and it seemed churlish to refuse, especially on such a lovely morning. She'd managed to give the impression that it was a working meeting, though she hadn't said what, and now, as Will comes to meet her, opening the garden gate to allow Bodger out, she's ready to avoid any kind of discussion.

'Hi,' she says brightly. 'Thanks, Will. Gosh, what an amazing day. Listen, I'm going down to the beach for a walk. Need to get some fresh air and exercise. See you both later.'

She gives him a wave, dashes into the house to collect Bodger's lead, drops her bag in the kitchen and hurries out again. Away from the house, she slows her stride, and tries to calm the chaos inside her head. Seeing Sebastian again has completely thrown her: she simply can't think straight. Sitting across the table from him, remembering times past, has unsettled her to an alarming degree. She takes deep, calming breaths, dropping her shoulders, willing herself back to normality. It's frightening that simply being there with him can have this effect on her. It's destabilizing all that is familiar and good in her life, undermining her loyalty, threatening everything with this crazy, fizzing sense of excitement.

Almost with relief she sees Leo, climbing the lane,

coming back from the beach, and she hails him, hoping for some kind of rescue from her thoughts. He's smiling as he approaches her, remembering the last time they met, almost at his gate.

'We'll have to stop meeting like this,' he says. 'May I offer you some refreshment? It's a bit late for coffee and a bit early for lunch. How about a drink?'

'Yes, please,' she answers fervently; so fervently, that they both burst out laughing.

They turn back together and go in at his gateway. Bodger follows obediently and Leo lets them all in and fills a bowl with water for him.

'The poor fellow's having a bit of a muddly day,' says Tessa, watching him drink. 'He's been in the garden with Will all morning and now I've rushed him out for a walk.'

Leo sets two glasses on the kitchen table, shows her the bottle and pours the wine.

'And is there any particular reason for rushing him out, or for your sudden overwhelming need for liquor?' asks Leo casually, pushing the glass in her direction as she sinks down in a chair at the table. 'You don't have to answer but I am the soul of discretion should you feel the need to let it all hang out.'

Tessa laughs again, feeling suddenly much calmer, grateful for his kindness.

'You wouldn't believe me if I told you. Can you imagine someone coming back unexpectedly into your life after years and years? It's totally crazy.'

She picks up her glass and sips the wine. The silence lengthens and she glances across the table. Leo is sitting quite still, turning his glass gently between his fingers, eyes narrowed in thought. Tessa turns more fully in her chair to look at him and he raises his head and smiles at her.

'It sounds . . . challenging?' he suggests, and raises his glass to her, and she smiles back, raising hers in response.

'All of that,' she agrees. 'You sound as if you know about it.'

Leo purses his lips, shakes his head. 'I have a slightly different problem. But I think it might be a bit unchivalrous to talk about it.'

Tessa is instantly intrigued. Thoughts of Sebastian recede slightly from the forefront of her mind and she leans forward.

'Oh, go on,' she says encouragingly. 'I promise I won't tell, and Bodger is also the soul of discretion.'

They look at Bodger, who is enjoying a handful of Bax's treats, and Leo grins. He takes another sip of wine and then seems to make up his mind.

'It's going to sound very silly, and very presumptuous, but here goes. You know my daughter-in-law, Bethany? Well, a friend of hers is staying in Dartmouth for a few weeks. Bethany invited her over when she was down, and since then there have been a couple of other meetings, and now I have this feeling that Em — that's her name, Emily — is beginning to get the idea that we might . . . well, become more friendly. I know it sounds crazy, especially as she's Bethany's age, but I've had a couple of texts suggesting we meet up.' He looks across at Tessa, embarrassed. 'Please don't think I'm the kind of man who goes round thinking young women are in love with him, but when you live alone there's a tendency . . . Oh God, what am I sounding like?'

He groans and puts his hand over his eyes as Tessa begins to laugh.

'That's tricky,' she agrees. 'Especially if she's Bethany's friend. What is she asking you to do?'

'She's suggested we go to Greenway and I slightly put her off by implying that Helen and George were still here. But I had a text just now asking if I can recommend the best place for walking on the cliffs.' He makes a little face. 'I mean, what can I say?'

'You could simply text 'Start Point'. But I see what you mean. It's hinting that you might like to show her in person.'

'Exactly. And I don't quite know how to handle it.'

Tessa watches him sympathetically. 'At least she didn't want to meet Helen and George.'

He hesitates, looks uneasy, and Tessa is reminded of his strange silence at the beginning when she talked about someone reappearing from the past.

'She's met them,' he says at last. 'We went over for coffee at the Royal Castle.'

She decides not to comment on this, but says instead: 'Well, hopefully she won't be around too long, but meanwhile perhaps it's a good plan not to be alone with her if you don't want to get her hopes up.'

He still looks as if there's something more on his mind than Bethany's friend and she decides to lighten the mood again.

'How about you introduce me to her,' she says, 'and let her draw her own conclusions?'

He begins to smile again, and she grins at him. 'Perhaps we should let her think you're a bit of a playboy?'

And now Leo does laugh. 'I think you've forgotten that she's Bethany's friend. Nobody's going to believe that. I'm afraid my reputation as a boring old stick-in-the-mud has gone before me.'

She shrugs. 'Sometimes it's our families who know

the least about us.'

And now it is she who suddenly becomes silent, thinking of Giles, and Henry and Charlotte, all totally unaware of Sebastian and the feelings he's reignited in her. Leo watches her thoughtfully.

'And you still haven't told me why you were so much in need of a drink,' he reminds her gently.

His gentleness disarms her and she heaves a huge sigh.

'It's nothing really. Just someone I loved when I was young unexpectedly reappearing and catching me a bit off balance.' She shakes her head. 'I'm being silly. Take no notice.'

'But that's actually a really big thing, isn't it?' He hesitates. 'I take it that you're talking about a man?'

She nods, her eyes on her glass. 'I was engaged to him when I met Giles. I'd known him when I was young. He was my best friend's glamorous elder brother and I utterly adored him. When I met Giles I realized that there are different kinds of love.' She tries to smile and takes a sip of wine. 'Relationships are hell, aren't they?'

He tops up her glass and touches it with his own. 'I'll drink to that,' he says.

★ ★ ★

'Was that Tessa?' asks Bea, coming out into the garden. 'I wonder if she wants anything from the farm shop.'

'She took Bodger and dashed off,' answers Will. 'Said she needed some fresh air and exercise.'

'Did she say where she'd been?'

Will shakes his head. 'She said she was going to

Dartmouth, which is why we had Bodger. She seemed a bit hyper, if you know what I mean.'

'Not as if she'd just been shopping?'

'She didn't have anything with her when she got out of the car. She just grabbed his lead and rushed off.'

Bea looked thoughtful. 'I wonder what she needed to do in Dartmouth. She went on Friday, didn't she?'

'Stop it,' Will says. 'You sound like some kind of policeman.'

Bea sighs. 'I'm just worried about her. This sudden change of mood. All this weekend she's been behaving as if she has a secret, an exciting one. She's behaving like a girl in love.'

They stare at each other, puzzled.

'But that's so unlike Tessa,' says Will, uncertainly. 'She's such a grounded sort of person. She loves her children and Giles.'

'But they're not here, are they?' Bea reminds him sharply.

'I wish they were,' says Will. 'We could do with Henry at the moment.'

He thinks with affection of Henry, who is always positive, hopeful, who calls them both 'Wilby', and whose presence would be good for them all.

Bea gives a little snort. 'We certainly don't need to distract him in the middle of exams. He'll be finding it difficult enough to concentrate as it is, if I know Henry.'

'I wish he had some idea of where he's going,' admits Will. 'But he's young yet. Plenty of time.'

'He needs a sense of direction,' says Bea firmly, who never likes to admit to the great affection she has for Henry lest it should spoil him. 'Too many friends and

distractions. Now, are you coming with me to Stokeley? If so, get a move on, it's nearly lunchtime.'

9

She watches Leo walking along the beach, hands in pockets, head bent; sees him climb the steps where the slipway used to be and disappear. He doesn't see her, standing at the back of the balcony, half hidden, and if he did he wouldn't recognize her. Instinctively she raises her hands to her head, gently smoothing the wispy white straggles of hair, growing back slowly after the chemo. Her wig, a tactful mix of her original golden brown and grey, is itchy and she wears it more so that other people shouldn't be embarrassed by her baldness than from any sense of vanity. Now that she's here, she can't bring herself to send that text, to tell him that she's staying in this house on the beach, which she booked on an impulse; in the hope that she might see him again.

Alice turns once more into the big room that stretches from the front to the back of the house and takes up most of the first floor. There, on the central mahogany table are the photographs. Her stepmother, Agnes, gave them to her after the funeral.

'I found these in your father's desk,' she said. 'I expect you'd like to have them.'

Now, Alice stands looking down at them, moving them gently, sliding them to see first this one and then that. Leo's mother, her aunt Heather, had always had extra copies printed for Alice and sent them on after the holidays, and it was a shock to see them again.

How poignant old photographs are, she thinks. How young we were. How careless and confident.

But more recent ones have drawn her attention. Family weddings in particular. Her father kept her in touch as the years passed and she knew that Leo was married and had two sons; that Helen and George had a son and a daughter; that Mags had twin girls. Alice picks up a photo of Leo at the marriage of his son James to a pretty girl and looks at it closely. It was a shock to see it after so many years, to see Leo as a middle-aged man with his arm around his son's shoulders, smiling at the camera. Would she have known him again? In her memories he's still the boy she knew, the young man of twenty whom she saw last at Helen's wedding. Helen is in the photograph, too. And George. George seems barely to have changed; the eternal Peter Pan with a few lines around his eyes and some grey streaks in his hair. Helen has settled calmly into middle-age but it's still possible to see the traces of the girl she once was.

Alice knew that Leo and his wife were separated, that he was now living at Long Orchard — her father had told her that much — and suddenly she longed to see him again. This photograph is at least ten years old and since then so much has happened: Jason's death, her battle with cancer. She puts the photograph down on the table and goes back to the balcony. The painted boards are gritty beneath her bare feet; she can smell the ozone, hear the cry of gulls. Gripping the balustrade, watching a small dinghy dancing on the shining water, she closes her eyes and raises her face to the sunshine. She hasn't come here to be morbid, to dwell on sad things or her own mortality. She has come to celebrate the past, to lay the ghosts of regret, and to repair the sins of omission. So why is she finding it so difficult to take the final step towards

Leo? She made the first move, booked the cottage, sent the text; why can't she now walk out on to the beach and say, 'Hello. Here I am'?

Once again she puts her hands to her fragile skull. Is it simply vanity that is preventing her? The dread of seeing Leo's look of surprise: of pity? Vanity made her ask for the wig to be made into a plait. She'd always kept her hair long, even as she grew old and it began to turn grey.

'Your hair is beautiful,' Jason had said. 'You must never cut it short.'

Her hands clutch the balustrade more tightly. How she misses him: his craziness, his passion for life, his delight in nature. He was her rock, right back to those first happy days in the commune in North Wales where she fled when she needed to hide. Nobody asked questions there; not till Jason.

'When's the baby due?' he asked her as they sat around the fire, some singing, some talking, others half asleep after a day working out in the winter's cold.

'In the spring,' she said. 'I shall have to move on soon. I'd be a liability here.'

Even now, standing in the warm May sunshine, she can remember the sense of terror at the thought of it.

Jason settled himself more comfortably beside her. She could feel his warmth against her arm, the comfort of it, and she wanted to say, 'Don't move. Don't go.'

'I heard this morning,' he was saying quietly, 'that the farmer up the valley needs some help. His farmhand's going and he's looking for someone. Nice little cottage. Nothing posh, but snug. I've told him I'm interested.'

She sat in silence, hugging her knees, wondering

if he were simply telling her or if he were suggesting something else. She liked Jason: he was kind, he grafted. He lost his way after university, travelled for a while, and now he's here: growing vegetables, chopping wood, and reciting poetry. Suddenly she knew that if he were to ask her to join him in the snug little cottage she'd go like a shot.

'That sounds nice,' she said, and smiled. 'Even if it's not posh.'

Her poshness was a tease between them, that her father was a brigadier. It gave Jason a chance to joke and make her laugh. But underneath there was always the kindness.

'So would you like to try it?' he asked. 'Give it a go?'

She looked at him then. 'Are you being serious? Me and the baby?'

'You and the baby,' he said. 'I can look after you both.'

His generosity overwhelmed her. It made her want to cry. 'But why would you do that?' she asked.

He touched her then, stroked her long plait of hair, and smiled. 'Just let's say that I can picture you in the bee-loud glade,' he said. 'But you have to promise one thing. That you'll never cut your hair off.'

She began to laugh, nestling against him, pushing her head into the warm angle of his neck.

'Never,' she promised. 'I'll always keep this plait, even when I'm old and grey.'

Alice wipes the tears from her cheeks, turns back into the house, climbs the stairs and goes into the bedroom. She strokes the thick grey-brown plait, lifts the wig from its stand on the old pine chest and puts it carefully on her head.

'Best I can do,' she says to Jason. 'So what do I do

next? I've lost my nerve.'

His photograph, in its small leather case, beams back at her. Here is a young Jason holding out a bunch of sweet peas, the first of the summer crop, grown in his potager all amongst the runner beans. Jason was a nurturer. He could encourage almost anything to grow, to bring things on; tending them, caring for them.

Including me and Adam, thinks Alice.

She remembers how she gazed down at the baby, feeling joy and terror, and a huge relief that he didn't look like George. He didn't look like anybody. Just a small, crumpled, rather red person. Jason was thrilled. He took this bundle into his arms and rocked him. They had prepared no names.

'Let's call him Adam,' said Jason.

She stared at them, too bewildered and weak from the long, difficult birth to disagree.

'Adam?'

She wondered if it might be a family name but Jason was grinning at her.

'World's first gardener,' he said. 'Great name.'

She agreed, just grateful that he hadn't suggested George. He'd never asked her about the baby's father. She'd told him that he was an old friend and it was a one-off moment after a party, and that she didn't want him to know. Jason accepted it calmly and took Adam to his heart. The tragedy was that there had been no more children. After Adam's difficult birth she was unable to have another. Jason took that in his stride, too. If he minded he never said so and everyone believed that Adam was his own child until, in time, it almost seemed as if it were true. But as Adam grew, Alice could see George's imprint. It was there

91

in his brown eyes and in the corners of his mouth, in his ability to wheedle himself out of trouble, and in his quick and clever mind. As she watched him grow, Alice knew that she could never show her family her son, especially the family at Long Orchard. She could never go back. A small part of her feels guilty that George doesn't know he has a clever, handsome son — or a beautiful granddaughter. Maya is Alice's joy and delight. She has been at school in England while her parents have been in New York, and she and Alice have grown very close. Adam and Maya have been the reasons why Alice has believed that she could never go back. Until last year, after her father died and she saw the photographs.

Now, Jason is dead and Adam is settled in New York and in the middle of a divorce, Maya is at university, and Alice is alone again. Now it might be safe to go back; to go home. So she wrote to Leo, careful not to put her address, only a mobile number, and waited. And he answered her: he invited her to come home.

So here she is, within a few hundred yards of Long Orchard, and having the biggest attack of cold feet that is possible to imagine. Because, of course, the danger isn't over. Even as she stood on the balcony on Saturday morning, screwing up her courage to walk out of the house and up the hill to Long Orchard, she saw them come down the steps and on to the beach: Leo, Helen and George. Even if she hadn't seen those wedding photographs she thinks she would have known them. Helen and Leo striding ahead, George slightly behind, glancing around him. Instinctively she drew back into the shadows, though she couldn't imagine that he would possibly recognize her. Foolishly she hurried upstairs and put her wig on, lest they might come suddenly knocking at the door and she would be caught, vulnerable, unprepared. How stupid she was not to imagine that Helen and George might be around. Perhaps they've retired here to be near to Leo.

'So what now?' she asks her reflection in the small tilting mirror. 'And does it matter?'

After all, George never knew she was pregnant, so why should she be fearful? It was always a risk but why lose her nerve now? But she knows why. It was seeing them so unexpectedly, the three of them walking across the beach so naturally, and she realized at that moment that thinking about coming back was one thing and the reality of it was another.

Yet she refuses to be deflected. She must regroup, gather up her courage and answer Leo's text. She must tell him that she is here and then leave it to him. Her original instinct was to reach out and she must hold fast to that. She looks again at Jason's photograph and remembers one of his favourite quotes:

Ah, but a man's reach should exceed his grasp,
Or what's a heaven for?

Seeing Leo just now, walking on the beach alone, was perhaps the moment to confront him. She's guessing that George and Helen were here for the weekend but, whatever the situation is, it's time to make the move. Nevertheless, she might suggest that the first meeting shall be here, on her territory, so that she can find out how the land lies. As she picks up her phone, takes a deep breath and goes back downstairs, she knows that she shouldn't have acted so rashly. She should have waited, made a sensible arrangement with Leo, not

93

just acted on impulse and turned up without warning him. Of course, Leo knows what she's like: surely he must remember that this spontaneous kind of behaviour was always part of her character. Still, arriving unannounced on his doorstep, despite his invitation, is too extreme.

Alice thinks carefully before she sends the text. I'm staying locally. Let me know a good time for us to meet. Alice x

She sits down in the wicker chair on the balcony, and waits for an answer.

10

In her tiny attic study, Bethany finishes the report she's writing and checks the messages on her phone. As she reads Em's latest email, Bethany's aware of a growing concern. Her old friend has always been a bit of a loose cannon — take this latest idea to leave her good job at an advertising agency and go on a sabbatical — but her latest messages are beginning to cause concern. To begin with, Em's attraction to Leo was slightly amusing, but dimly Bethany can begin to see danger looming. Supposing, just supposing, Leo has taken a fancy to her old friend, and that they should begin to form a close friendship? Em is volatile and needy — and very attractive. Perhaps Leo, with old age approaching, might find the idea of a companion a good one; perhaps he's had enough of being alone. Bethany is feeling guilty now; guilty that she slightly encouraged Em's silly emails, allowing her to assume that Bethany was encouraging her, rather than just the whole thing being a bit of holiday fun: a joke.

Bethany's imagination takes another leap forward. Should Leo and Em become an item, how would that change their own visits to Long Orchard? Those free holidays by the sea are very nice. And what might happen to James's inheritance? She suddenly remembers that Em told her that Leo had taken Helen and George to meet her in Dartmouth. Why would he do that?

Sitting there at her desk, Bethany is filled with an irrational alarm. Men can be very susceptible, especially to a much younger woman. And Em sounds very sincere in her desire to attract him. But what can she do? Em has asked her not to tell James, which she wouldn't want to do just yet — and there's no way she could confront her father-in-law — but still the alarm bells are ringing.

An idea occurs to her. It's slightly crazy, probably completely over the top, but she knows that there is one person who might be able to deal with this without too much fall-out. Without giving herself time to change her mind, Bethany dials her mother-in-law's number.

'Hello, Bethany.'

Jenny's voice is cool. She doesn't question, ask if everyone is OK, comment on the weather. She simply waits. Bethany starts to panic. She was going to suggest that they might meet up, but she can imagine that Jenny won't want to schlep into central London from her delightful flat in Blackheath, and she loses her nerve.

'Hi,' she says uncertainly. 'Hi, Jenny. I was just . . . I mean, I thought I'd phone . . . ' How effective silence is. 'The thing is . . . '

Bethany now knows that she's being a complete idiot. She cannot think how she can broach this subject without it sounding utterly ridiculous.

'Are you going to tell me what the thing is, Bethany?'

'It sounds crazy,' says Bethany miserably.

'Clearly you thought it was worth telephoning me, so suppose you let me judge how crazy it is. Is it to do with someone or something?'

'It's to do with Leo,' blurts Bethany.

'Leo?' At last there is a hint of emotion in Jenny's

voice: a slight surprise. 'Is there something wrong with Leo?'

'No,' says Bethany quickly, 'not wrong. Oh God, this sounds so weird now I'm saying it out loud but it's to do with my friend Em. I think you've met her. She's staying at my parents' little bolt hole in Dartmouth for a few weeks and I introduced her to Leo, and they've met up a couple of times and now she's, well, she's getting a bit silly about him.'

'Silly?'

'Yes. You know. Emotional.'

'You mean she thinks she's falling in love with him?'

Jenny's voice is still cool but Bethany feels calmer now and is able to pull herself together.

'Yes. And I don't know how to put a bit of a brake on it. I mean, she's so much younger and, well . . . '

Bethany begins to flounder and, when she eventually speaks, Jenny sounds amused.

'You think that Leo might lose his head and James might lose his inheritance, and you don't want a stepmother-in-law of your own age living in at Long Orchard when you go down on holiday?'

'OK. It sounds silly when you put it like that,' says Bethany rather sulkily, 'but, actually, yes.'

'I agree with you,' says Jenny briskly. 'Leo and I are still married but he owns Long Orchard and if there's anything left at the end of the day I want it to go to my sons, not to that rather odd young woman that I met at one of your parties. I think it's very wise of you to be wary.'

'Right,' says Bethany, when she can speak. 'Good. Fine. But what can we do?'

'I'll go down,' answers Jenny. 'I'll message Leo and tell him I'd like to stay for a few days.'

'What, just like that? Out of the blue?'

'Why not? It's the Bank Holiday this weekend. I'll go a few days early to avoid the traffic. You know that Leo and I stay with each other. It's all part of the deal. We all stay with Leo. Helen and George were there last week.'

'I know,' says Bethany, still slightly in shock by this response. 'He took them to meet Em.'

There is a little silence and she can almost hear Jenny processing this information.

'Did he?' she says at last. Her voice is thoughtful. 'Rather odd of him. Very well. I'll probably drive down on Wednesday. Obviously you won't tell your friend, or Leo, that we've had this conversation.'

'Of course not. And you won't say anything to Leo, will you? That I've told you about Em, I mean?'

'Certainly not. Will you let me know if there's anything else I need to know before I go?'

'I feel a bit of a cow,' says Bethany. 'I mean, it's like sneaking on someone, isn't it?'

'I've already told you that I think you're being very sensible. If I remember your friend as well as I think I do, I can only say that Leo would make her very unhappy. Do you know if she plans to meet up with him in the next few days?'

'Not for certain, but I think she's working on it. She says he's being very kind and sweet to her but I suspect that really it's just Leo being chivalrous.'

'Well, that's one word for it,' says Jenny, briskly. 'Keep me in the loop. Goodbye, Bethany.'

Bethany sits quite still, picturing her mother-in-law's smooth steely grey hair, and her steely grey eyes. She wonders how Jenny will deal with the situation and she feels rather sorry for Leo. And for poor Em.

Quickly she begins to message her friend. She knows that Em is expecting comfort and encouragement in her emotional state, but Bethany can't bring herself to write about it. She knows she's been disloyal and she feels guilty. Instead she writes about plans for half-term, James's promotion, and hopes that she'll get away with it until Jenny arrives on the scene and takes control.

★ ★ ★

Leo is slightly surprised at how much he's enjoyed talking to Tessa. Probably because he grew up with two elder sisters and a strong-minded mother he's always been comfortable in the company of women. He's used to them telling him what to do, taking charge of him, mocking his indecisiveness. His nickname, 'Lion', was always a tease, simply because it was so clear that he wasn't one. In retrospect it was clear that he was attracted to Jenny because she was familiar to him, she was like all the women he knew, and she simply carried the role forward into marriage until they both agreed, once the boys went off to university, that it was time to separate. They are still good friends, though. And that sums it up. Women like him because he isn't a threat. He's always the little brother: kind, undemanding, reliable.

Leo wonders about this man who is threatening Tessa's peace of mind; what he must be like. It's a coincidence that they should both be in a similar situation: revenants turning up unexpectedly. He didn't mention Alice but simply allowed Tessa to talk, listening while she explained her sense of loss for the cove, how she missed her children, empty-nest syndrome, as if she needed some kind of justification for having been taken unawares by this ex-lover.

'Thanks for listening, Leo,' she said when she got up to go. 'I'm just being a complete prat. And I never asked you about your own problem.'

'Next time,' he promised, smiling as she reached up to kiss him. 'We'll be prats together. And I promise you I'm an expert. I can out-prat you anytime.'

She laughed, encouraged Bodger to his feet and Leo went to the gate with them, waving them off up the lane.

Now, as he wanders up through the garden, along the grassy path that borders the wildflower meadow, he wonders if he could ever bring himself to tell Tessa about Alice. The difficulty, of course, is that it isn't just his secret. She isn't simply a cousin returning after years away; there are complications. Even now, amidst all his anxieties, the scene around him claims his attention and he looks with delight at the tapestry of colour — cornflowers, lady's smocks, campion, poppies, celandine — and shades his eyes to locate the swift, screaming overhead, slicing the air like a blue-grey bullet. The thorn trees, pink and white, are massed with blossom and Leo dreads that 'rough winds do shake the darling buds of May', knowing how swiftly the weather can change, how the calm, still air can seem to buckle, shudder, as the storm sweeps in from the south-west.

For some reason this makes him think of Jenny and he takes his phone from his pocket. There are three messages. Disbelievingly Leo stares at them. The first is from Em.

Sudden thought, Leo. How about coming over for coffee one morning? Em

The second message is from Jenny.

Hi Leo. I'm thinking of coming down for the Bank Holiday. I'd probably travel down on Wednesday. I know you've already had a few visitors lately and that the boys aren't coming so I hope that you won't be booked up! I'll bring supplies, as usual. Jenny xx

The third is from Alice.

I'm staying locally, Leo. Let me know a good time to meet. Alice x

He reads the second two messages again. It's almost the worst complication he could have imagined. The last person that he wants to see at the moment is Jenny. However calmly he explains that Alice is a long-lost cousin, Leo just knows that she will see through any subterfuge, and he also knows how difficult it will be to pretend, to prevaricate, under that cool grey glance. He thinks about Alice, her vulnerability, and wonders how she would cope. He knows there will be questions from Jenny: why has she stayed away so long? Where has she been? Is she married? Does she have children? He can remember when his boys were young, coming back from school, from weekends away, and hearing them murmur: 'OK. Here we go. Third degree coming up.'

Alice wouldn't last two minutes under Jenny's interrogation techniques, but what can he do? How to explain to her? He looks again at the texts. Jenny could be here by Wednesday lunchtime so he must act quickly.

He sees Em's text again and groans aloud.

As usual he has been naïve in thinking that Alice could return without any kind of drama. He wonders how much she knows about his own marriage, and once again he feels the familiar guilt that he allowed her to vanish so completely. Yet it was clear that Alice hadn't wanted to be found. Uncle Philip talked of his occasional meetings with her, usually in London, in cafés and coffee bars, where she remained elusive, secretive, the same old Alice. But now she is here, staying locally.

Leo sits down on the little bench at the top of the meadow and begins to plan his strategy. He must try to hold everything together for Alice without letting her feel sidelined, whilst not allowing Jenny to become suspicious. The timescale here is difficult. Meanwhile it is possible that, in Em's case, Jenny might be a positive factor. He remembers how, when they were children, his sisters used to call him Lionheart after the crusader king — though there was always the element of mockery, the little jokes. They still hurt, the eggshells in the compost, still sharp and painful, making him feel inadequate. He knows he should have the courage to tell Jenny that she can't come, to invite Alice to stay, to tell Em that she's got the wrong idea about him. But he knows that he won't: he'll try to keep everyone happy.

Sitting in the sunshine, Leo begins to tap out his messages.

11

As she walks away up the lane with Bodger, Tessa is thinking about how much she likes Leo. She's known him for years, of course, and has always been fond of him, but this morning it's as if she's seen him in a new light. Not only as a friendly neighbour, Will's chess partner, a father and grandfather welcoming his children home at regular intervals, but as Leo in his own right. A funny, kind, understanding man.

And a rather attractive one, she thinks, as she stands aside, calling to Bodger to sit, as a Land Rover passes along the lane. She waves to the driver, smiling as he shouts a greeting, and walks on, still thinking about Leo. He was so responsive that the age gap — because, after all, she is roughly the same age as his own boys — seemed totally irrelevant. It was like telling her troubles to a close and trusted friend. She remembers the last time she met him in the lane and he invited her in. They had coffee and talked about gardening. It was good, and now she feels that she's built on that earlier moment. Tessa can't quite decide why she feels so buoyant, as if she's discovered an over-looked treasure amongst some old, well-loved bits and pieces. She laughs at herself, wondering if it's meeting Sebastian again that has given her this rather delightful boost, this much-needed mental swing from depression to an almost euphoric joyfulness.

Everything has taken on a new glow. That lake of bluebells glimmering beneath the newly green-tipped trees, those paint-bright celandines spilling along the ditch, the swallows swooping from the old barn: it's as if she's never really noticed them before.

When a text pings in, she pauses to check her phone whilst Bodger waits patiently. It's from Sebastian.

Missing you already, kiddo. X

Tessa grins. She's enjoying herself so much. But she won't answer straight away, mustn't look too keen. Fleetingly she wonders whether Leo's wine is giving her this light-headed sensation. Whatever it is, it's different and it's fun, and she means to make the most of it.

Bea and Will are just back from a farm shop run as she and Bodger arrive home. She greets them enthusiastically, offers to carry shopping and invites them in for some lunch.

'You seem in high spirits,' comments Bea casually.

'I've just been having a glass of wine with Leo,' Tessa answers. After all, there's no reason not to tell them. It's not a secret. 'I met him on the walk. Great fun. So how about it? I could rustle up some soup?'

They accept and, while they finish unpacking the shopping and putting things away, she goes into her own kitchen to prepare for this impromptu lunch. Still on a high, she throws caution to the wind and replies to Sebastian's message.

Same time, same place tomorrow, if you're still around? X

She pours some fresh water for Bodger, puts some rolls to warm in the Rayburn and begins to prepare the soup.

★   ★   ★

104

Bea is staring at Will with her eyebrows raised.

'Leo?' she says questioningly.

Will is putting things into the freezer, surprised by Tessa's remark and still obscurely concerned by these new high spirits.

'Nothing wrong with having a drink with Leo,' he answers. 'After all, why not? She's known him for years.'

'Nothing at all,' agrees Bea briskly, 'but I'm assuming Tessa didn't meet him in Dartmouth, and you said she was in this excitable mood when she came back and rushed off with Bodger.'

Will sighs. Part of him doesn't want to get involved with this, but another part is concerned by the sudden change. He feels uneasy talking about Tessa in this way but he agrees with Bea that it's worrying. Tessa is behaving rather like someone who has fallen suddenly and delightfully in love. She's on a different plane, and he can think of no other reason for her odd behaviour.

'I suppose,' he says reluctantly, 'that they might have met by chance in Dartmouth and he said, 'Come round for a drink when you get home,' but why didn't she simply tell me that instead of saying that she needed exercise and fresh air? We all know Leo. It wouldn't be world-shattering if he invited her for a drink, would it?'

'No,' answers Bea thoughtfully. 'What is unusual is her reaction to it.'

Will finishes his task and turns to look at her.

'I trust you're not going to mention this when we go round for lunch?'

'No,' says Bea, rather unwillingly. 'No, of course not. But some instinct is telling me that things aren't right. I'm not going to stand by and see any harm come to that little family, Will. I know that Tessa misses the cove the most of all of us, she's trying to adjust to both the children being gone, and now Giles is off on this assignment. She's vulnerable.'

'I hear what you say,' answers Will, 'and of course I agree with you, but you can't possibly suspect Leo of doing anything that might do damage to them. He's very fond of Giles.'

'I know,' sighs Bea. 'I know all that. But I still can't help worrying. Oh, come on. Let's go and have that lunch.'

★ ★ ★

Tessa is tapping a message on her phone as they come into the kitchen. She's smiling to herself, her eyes bright. She glances up at them and she looks so much like a naughty child that Bea has to control all her ex-matron instincts to prevent her from saying: 'Give me that!' Instead, she says: 'Will brought a bottle in case you are still in a drinking mood.'

Tessa laughs, happiness radiating from her, and stretches out her hand to take it.

'Thank you,' she says. 'What a nice idea. We could add some to the soup. Or is it just sherry that you add to soup?'

'Neither,' responds Will smartly. 'Terrible waste of perfectly good wine. I'll have mine neat, thank you.'

Bea is trying to think of a good way to lead the conversation back to Leo but Tessa is there before her.

'I don't often have a drink in the middle of the day,' she says, 'but it was rather a nice change. Of course it's different when there's someone else, isn't it? Not

106

so much fun on one's own.'

'Was he celebrating something?' asks Bea casually, receiving her glass.

'No, he said that it was a bit late for coffee and a bit too early for lunch, so a drink seemed a good option. He was just coming up from the beach.'

Bea gives Will a little glance. So that answers the question about whether Tessa had met Leo in Dartmouth.

'We must get together for another game of chess,' says Will. 'We could invite him for supper. You could join us, Tessa, if you'd like that?'

'I'd love to,' she answers, putting out the bowls of soup, and taking the rolls from the oven. 'It was rather fun just to sit and chat with him. It's getting to be a habit. Only it was coffee last time. We talked about gardening. Leo has always seemed very self-contained, the tiniest bit distant, but just lately I've felt more at ease with him.'

Bea breaks her roll and picks up her spoon. Tessa doesn't speak about Leo as if she's fallen in love with him, which is a relief, but it still leaves the question of who it might be — if it's the case. Will is asking Tessa for news of Giles, and of Henry and Charlotte, and Tessa talks easily and naturally about them all. But when Will tells her that he and Bea will be going to Totnes tomorrow morning, and suggests that they might all go and have lunch in the town, her ease of manner falters.

'Oh,' she says. 'Tomorrow. I don't think I can . . .'

She hesitates, looking embarrassed, but neither Will nor Bea hasten to help her out. They wait politely, eating their soup, until she gives a little laugh.

'It's no good,' she says ruefully. 'Totally gone out of

my head but I know there's something on tomorrow. Probably coffee with a chum or something.'

'That's a pity,' Will says politely. 'Another time, then.'

But all Bea's fears are resurrected. She remembers how Tessa looked, sending the message on her phone, as they came into the kitchen, and all her instincts tell her that this is the reason why Tessa can't join them tomorrow. She has a secret and Bea admits she won't rest until she knows what it is.

'So not Leo, then,' she says when she and Will are back in their own quarters.

Will grimaces; he pulls down the corners of his mouth and raises his eyebrows in a kind of facial shrug.

'What?' demands Bea. 'What's that face supposed to mean?'

'I'm just thinking that if Tessa has suddenly developed something more than a long-term affection for him it's a very clever way to put us off the scent.'

'And you seriously believe that she's that devious?'

'All women are devious,' he answers, provokingly, 'but I agree that it's not like Tessa.'

'Invite him over for a game of chess,' says Bea. 'That was a good idea of yours. And then we'll ask Tessa in for a drink while he's here.'

'How ruthless you are,' says Will admiringly. 'But could I bear the stress of it? I know your methods, Sherlock.'

'Just do it,' says Bea.

12

Em stares at Leo's text with dismay. This is the last thing she expected.

> Thanks for the invitation, Em. Jenny's down for the Bank Holiday. Perhaps you'd like to come over some time and say hello. Leo

She can remember that Bethany explained the odd relationship Leo and Jenny have, but it hasn't occurred to Em that Jenny might come down to visit when the rest of the family weren't staying, too. Or maybe they are. Maybe James's brother and his family are coming, too. But surely Bethany would have mentioned it? Em feels confused and upset. She's been building a little scenario around Leo, almost as if she's inventing a little world here in this magical place, and she can't bear to see it shattered by a cold blast of reality. It's impossible to imagine sitting around Leo's table with Jenny watching her with that direct gaze of hers without feeling uncomfortable. And why should Leo suggest it? It was one thing going over when Bethany and James were there, but this is weird, unless . . .

Em is suddenly seized by a new idea. Perhaps this is Leo's way of making sure she knows the whole family. After all, he brought Helen and George to Dartmouth to meet her, and now he's suggesting that she should meet Jenny. He probably doesn't know they've already met at Bethany's party. Why should he? No, he is trying to bring her into his family circle, making her a part of it, in his own gentle way.

This thought restores her confidence and raises her

spirits. Leo is a kind, quiet man: he won't want to rush into anything and risk upsetting people. Once again she reviews all his little acts and words that indicate his feelings for her, and now she can see this last text as a positive thing. She remembers the negative things that Jenny said to Bethany after that party — that Em's dear old dad was a luvvie and that her family was like something out of Nancy Mitford — and she wonders if Jenny will repeat these to Leo. She can't wait to tell Bethany this new development. What will she make of it?

Em experiences a distinct thrill of pleasure at the prospect of turning up at Leo's place as a close friend of the family and giving Jenny a bit of a shock. Smiling to herself, she texts back to Leo.

That would be great. Let me know when. Em x

She presses Send and gives the air a little punch. Bring it on.

★ ★ ★

Alice stares at Leo's text with dismay. This is the last thing she's expected.

My wife, Jenny, is unexpectedly coming to stay on Wednesday for the Bank Holiday. Let me know if you'd like to meet before then. Where are you staying?

It's a shock to see the reference to his wife. Over a period of years, during those uncomfortable meetings with her father, Alice discovered that Leo was married, that they had two sons, and later that Leo had moved to Long Orchard and his wife had gone to London. The implication was that this was a separation, perhaps even a divorce, and this wife had never for a moment entered into Alice's calculations

110

when she impulsively returned here, to the home of her childhood. Of course his family might visit him, indeed George and Helen already have, but a wife is a different thing altogether.

Alice walks out on to her balcony, anxious and confused. How can she possibly meet up with Leo in these circumstances: a brief meeting fitted in before his wife turns up at Long Orchard? How could it be done? This isn't a casual meeting of old friends — a cup of coffee in the little café along the front, or a drink in the pub. She realizes how much she's been building into this meeting, how she's been looking towards Leo as someone to tether her to this lonely, frightening world, and she feels the old familiar panic rising; the need to run away, to disappear.

She stares out across the sea. Storm clouds are beginning to pile up along the horizon. The wind has been rising and tall, glassy-green waves are racing in, white-topped, curling and smashing against the rocks. She watches, feeling all her own emotions in that turbulence. She can't simply fit in a meeting with Leo, but what should she do now? It was a huge risk coming here, so close to him. She might have met him unexpectedly at any moment — on the beach, in the little shop, getting into the car. Yet the risk was somehow exciting, taking them both off guard, and sweeping them back to the past. And that was assuming that he recognized her.

Instinctively Alice puts her hands to her head, smoothing and stroking the wisps of white hair. How vulnerable her skull feels; how tender. Deep down she requires Leo to see her like this: to acknowledge it and still to love her. It has become essential for her wellbeing to believe that this will happen. But not in a brief meeting hastily fitted in before the arrival of his wife. Alice wonders if Leo realizes that, through her father, she's kept in touch, and knows about his life. The casual use of the phrase 'My wife, Jenny' tells her nothing — except that his wife still holds an important place in his life.

Alice turns back inside, picks up her phone and rereads his text. She wonders what he would say if she told him that she was staying not much more than a five-hundred-yard walk away, but she lacks the courage. She texts quickly:

I don't think that will work. I'll be in touch.

A x

She presses Send and stands still, trying to control her panic. Her whole instinct is willing her to run away — but where can she go?

★ ★ ★

Leo stares at the texts with dismay. This is the last thing he's expected.

That would be great. Let me know when. E x

I don't think that will work. I'll be in touch.

A x

Each of these is the exact opposite of what he thought would be the response. He imagined that Em would back right off and that Alice would want to make contact before Jenny arrived. Leo stares blankly at his phone and then groans aloud. He's got it wrong again. Completely misjudged the situation. Clearly Em has merely been behaving in a friendly way, has no designs on him whatever, and is regarding him simply as her best friend's pa-in-law. Remembering how he confided in Tessa, he groans again at his vanity. And now he will be obliged to invite Em over, or meet her somewhere with Jenny. Complications abound.

And as for Alice . . . Well, in this case he feels anxious. He found it difficult to word the text and knows that he's been clumsy. He forgets sometimes that they haven't seen each other for over forty years. He's fairly confident, from his conversations with Uncle Philip, that Alice would know his situation, just as he knows that she lived in Wales and later moved to somewhere near Oxford, and that there was a man in her life but they weren't married. There was no mention of a child. Some instinct makes him guess that she is here alone, which is all the more reason for locating her. But how? He's tried phoning her mobile but she never answers it, or the messages he leaves for her. His frustration is overwhelming. With a terrible clarity he can see the pattern reforming: Alice confiding in him, his procrastination, and then her flight.

But, he argues with himself defensively, I'm not procrastinating this time. I asked her to meet me.

Yes, answers his alter ego, but implying that it will be squashed in before your wife arrives for the Bank Holiday.

He can't think now why he mentioned Jenny. Wasn't it simply to indicate that there was some urgency to planning a meeting before he would be distracted? Perhaps he should have simply given a time and a date for tomorrow and left it at that. And why hasn't she told him where she is? 'Staying locally' could mean anything. Knowing Alice, it might be a B & B, or a caravan on the beach at Beesands. Unbidden, a memory flows out of the corners of his mind.

A starry, starry night fifty years ago. They lay on their backs, side by side on the beach, gazing up at the universe, which seemed to be gently turning itself inside out: dazzling white diamonds against a black velvet background. Beneath their hands and bare legs the stones were still warm from baking all day in the hot sunshine. He felt her thin fingers reaching for his, holding them tight, her voice barely a whisper.

'We'll always be together, won't we, old Lion?'

He clasped her small hand, smiling in the darkness.

'Of course we will. We'll have a B & B right here on the beach. You can do the cooking and I'll take the guests sailing in the dinghy.'

They'd talked about this many times.

Her hand clutched his more tightly.

'Promise?'

He was nearly thirteen and she was eleven.

An upstairs window slams shut as the wind gets up, shattering the memory. Quickly Leo seizes his phone and begins to text:

Why can't we meet tomorrow? Please tell me where you're staying. L x

He presses Send and stares at the screen, willing her to respond. But it remains blank and presently he puts it in his pocket and sits down to wait.

* * *

The storm races in, the rain streaming across the surface of the sea, clattering on roofs, smashing fragile blossoms. Swaying and blowing, glassy curtains of water obscure the headlands, driven by the wind. It falls on the new-mown fields so that they resemble soaked rugs of gold. It fills small streams, which overflow and rush into dry ditches, which pour into the rivers that lead back to the sea.

13

Sebastian is the first to arrive at Bayards Cove. Checking that Tessa isn't in the café, he walks out on to the quay, looking downriver to the castle, and beyond to the sea. The storm has passed, leaving the town bedraggled in its wake but enjoying the sunny morning. Chairs and tables are being set back on the pavements, dinghies are being baled out; up on a balcony a man is rearranging plant pots.

The lower ferry has arrived at the slip and cars are driving off, and a naval cutter passes abeam, heading out to sea. Sebastian watches it, wondering if his son is on board, and quickly turns away: Nick thinks his father is back in London. Someone else is standing at the quay rail: a woman wearing a long skirt with a loose patchwork jacket and a headscarf tied at the back of her neck. She has a rather charming bohemian look and though she is not his type, he smiles at her because it is his nature to be friendly.

'Quite a storm,' he observes. 'Glad I wasn't at sea.'

She returns his smile and he sees now that she's older than he guessed. Her clothes have misled him but she must have been very pretty once, back in the day. He smiles again and walks across the cobbles to the café. He reaches the door and here is Tessa, hurrying towards him. As she laughs and they hug, he feels all sorts of sensations and is glad to be swept inside, to go through the process of finding a table and ordering, so that he has chance to recover a little.

The divorce has battered him, leaving him humiliated. It is a blow to his pride that it should be Liz who met someone else, that she should leave him. It was he who had the reputation for being flirtatious, for enjoying the company of women — though he had never been unfaithful — and his wife's infidelity was a huge shock.

It is good to be here with Tessa, to see that responsive glint, the delight in his company that she is unable to hide. It's a shock, too, to find that those old feelings for her are still there. Whether it was the real thing, he's never been able to decide. Whether it was his own prevarication or her meeting Giles, it is impossible to look back and know precisely how their love ended. Before the wedding could be arranged, he was posted to Washington, and somehow everything came to a halt. Certainly he wasn't able to see himself living in that cove with her two quaint old cousins. That wasn't his style at all, and it was another reason for drawing back from the commitment.

Sebastian smiles at Tessa across the table. He doesn't want to think about all that, he simply wants to sit here with her, enjoying her company, having fun.

★   ★   ★

Tessa smiles back at him. There's something so invigorating in all this: making sure that Bea and Will set off for Totnes, willing them to hurry lest she should be late. And, at last, once the car disappeared, settling Bodger with his water bowl full and a few treats. She drove quickly, but not too quickly in case she should catch them up, glad that the storm was over, noting, with this new heightened awareness, the damaged

116

blossom, grass bright as emerald, the sky a bright, new-rinsed blue.

She found a parking place, locked the car, and hurried through the town, heart racing. And there he was, almost at the door, looking so pleased to see her that she couldn't resist hugging him before they went inside. Now they sit waiting for their coffee, smiling at each other, and she feels slightly foolish. After all, he's just an old friend, though rather a special one, and it's silly to be behaving like a teenager, but somehow she can't help herself. It's as if she's being offered all the joy of being young again, of being free to be herself. Not mother of Henry and Charlotte, not wife of Giles nor the carer of Bea and Will, but just herself, Tessa.

She resists the pang of guilt; she doesn't want to think about all that. She just wants to be here, listening to the jazzy music and the sounds of the coffee machines and the banter of the baristas, and to feel alive and happy, here with Sebastian.

★ ★ ★

From her corner, Em watches them. She wonders what the relationship can be; how it is that two middle-aged people, a man and a woman, can take time off to meet here simply, by the look of them, to have fun. She wonders if they've met on a dating site. They have a look about them that indicates that they're not just good friends, yet they have none of the lovers' habit of holding hands, touching, gazing soulfully into each other's eyes. It's just a strange kind of excitement that she can't quite pin down, though she knows that Ruskin would be urging her to do so. 'Does a man die at your feet . . .'

Reluctantly, Em draws her laptop towards her and opens it. She's been thinking too much about the proposed meeting with Leo and Jenny to be able to concentrate much on her work. And even now, she checks her emails before she opens her work folder. Nothing much going on, no response from Bethany about this amazing new development, and Em feels slightly let down. She needs her friend's input, her collaboration, to be able to enjoy all this to the full.

Disappointed, Em opens the work file and stares at its sparse contents. Why should it all be so difficult? She stares around her for inspiration: at the couple who are now roaring with laughter at some private joke, at the group of mums and children on the sofas by the wood-burner, at the elderly man with his newspaper, and at a woman who has just come in, rather boho, long cotton skirt, silk scarf tied around her head in gypsy style. Nothing here to inspire her, to give life to her play.

As she stares at the screen, her mind drifts back to Leo, and she is seized with an idea. Why shouldn't Leo bring Jenny here to meet her, on Em's patch rather than at Long Orchard? That could come later, depending on how long Jenny stays. Before she can lose her nerve, Em reaches for her phone, scrolls to Leo's number and begins to text.

Hi Leo. I expect you know Bayards Cove Café in Dartmouth. How about you and Jenny meeting me here for coffee before the Bank Holiday kicks off? E x

She sends the text and sits back, pleased with this idea. She'll feel more confident here, for that first meeting of them all together. Abandoning any idea of work, she closes the file and begins to send another email to Bethany.

118

Alice orders a hot chocolate and chooses a table next to a man sitting alone, doing a crossword. This is as far as she has got in her plan to run away. The storm put a stop to any immediate departure and by the time it was over, it was dark and too late. Even by morning she had no idea where to go, but, still in a panic, she packed an overnight bag, got into the car and drove the familiar road to Dartmouth.

Parking the car on the Embankment, she walked around the town and out on to the quay at the cove, wondering what she should do next. She watched the man, who spoke to her in such a friendly way about the storm, meet a woman and go into the café by the Dartmouth Arms pub, and after a moment she decided to try it for herself. It has a busy, friendly atmosphere, and it's a relief to sit here, unnoticed and unknown, to try to relax and make a plan. She's already noticed the sign up on the wall advertising a room to let, and she's wondering whether to lie low here until Leo's wife has gone. She has a horror of meeting them unexpectedly in the village, or on the beach, although she wonders if Leo would even recognize her. She's decided not to wear the wig, which makes her look much younger, but simply to wear the soft, silk scarf and let people make their own assumptions.

Meanwhile she feels safe here, tucked away in this corner of Dartmouth — Leo and his family always used to go to the Royal Castle — and it will give her time to think, to plan.

14

Jenny turns off the A38, heading towards Dartmouth, driving through the familiar lanes, passing the landmarks she knows so well. She's aware of the countryside around her: small neat fields, steep wooded valleys, round medieval hills dotted with heraldic sheep, and in the distance, the high slopes of the moor. She can understand why Leo loves this place and once, way back, she hoped that she would grow to love it, too, just as she hoped that her love for Leo would grow. She knows now that it was a young woman's idealistic dream — Leo was so loving, so eager to share his passion for this place with her — the desire to fulfil the role of wife and mother, to be like her friends.

As she drives up the hill, bypassing Totnes, glancing across at the castle on the hill, Jenny remembers how happy she was when she became pregnant. Surely it would establish her firmly in that role and fill the emptiness, the sense of something missing in her life. And she was happy. She loved her children, and she loved Leo, but the emptiness remained. Even the regular dashes to London, to see her friends, to catch up, didn't fill the need. And then she met Eliza, and suddenly everything became clear.

'But why?' she asked, dazed, frightened by these new emotions. 'Why did it take me so long?'

'You were in denial,' Eliza answered. 'You were determined to be the perfect wife and mother so you were always looking in the wrong direction.'

They agreed that they must wait, put their love on

hold until the boys left school, and then Jenny would tell Leo the truth and move back to London. It would be difficult enough to come out in London amongst all her friends, but to do it in a small Devon village would have been impossible for her; impossible to face her colleagues in the staffroom or the parents. But the hardest thing of all, she thought, would be telling Leo. Their married life had very quickly settled into a companionable relationship, more like a brother and sister, in which she had quickly taken the leading role. He was used to that, of course, but occasionally she would surprise him looking at her, puzzled, rather wistful, and she felt an odd kind of guilt that she could experience none of the passion that she imagined was present in her friends' marriages. Though, to be fair to herself, Leo was too self-contained, too quiet to be blown away by great passion.

When she told him, after the initial shock she was aware of an odd expression on his face. A moment passed and then she recognized it as relief and she realized that he'd imagined that the fault was his, that he was unable to fulfil her needs, to make her happy, and impulsively she put her arms around him and held him close.

'Sorry,' she muttered. 'I'm so sorry, Leo.'

He held her for a few moments, then gently let her go. They talked for a long while and even now, twenty years on, she still feels a sense of gratitude, remembering how they managed it. She told Leo that she didn't want the boys to know yet, but once they were both away from home it shouldn't be too difficult. She would apply for a teaching post she coveted at a school in London, she would be discreet, and she and Leo would remain close friends. She continued to live alone — she preferred it that way — and as the years passed she realized that she was not cut out to live in a close relationship with anyone. She liked her own space and freedom. As for Leo, it seemed that he felt much the same way; they were two of a kind and he seemed content to live alone, happy in his work, busy with his projects on his land. The boys, busy with their own lives, accepted this kind of formal separation; the family still worked happily together, whether in London or Devon, and there were no fights or arguments.

Driving between Devon banks of ash and thorn, glimpsing the sparkle of the distant sea, Jenny thinks about this new complication. She has no intention of allowing that rather odd friend of Bethany's to creep under Leo's guard and insinuate herself into his life, but there's the faint chance that Leo might, at this late date, have fallen in love and Jenny needs to be sure. She has no right to interfere but she cannot imagine them in a serious relationship. She turns on to the coast road, heading for Long Orchard and for Leo.

★ ★ ★

Leo hears the car pull in and goes out to meet her. She's still so slim, in her jeans and loose shirt, her grey hair cut into a neat swinging bob, that she has a youthful look and he is reminded of the long-ago Jenny who mistook a longing for love and a need to be like her girlfriends for the belief that she was in love with him. Although she's retired from teaching she's still on the board of governors and heads up several charitable institutions. Leo definitely wouldn't want to mess with her, and the thought makes him smile as he opens his arms for a hug.

'What?' she says, as she returns his embrace. 'What are you grinning at?'

'Nothing,' he answers. 'I'm not. So to what do I owe this unexpected visit?'

She pulls her bag from the back seat and passes it to him.

'Do I have to have a reason?'

He shrugs. 'You usually do. It's not like you to be impulsive. You like everything organized down to the last detail.'

'How dull you make me sound,' she says, following him into the house. 'Am I really that boring?'

'You know you are. So what would you like to drink? Tea? Coffee?'

All the time he's bantering with her, Leo is praying that Alice will not suddenly arrive. It's his biggest nightmare that she will take him by surprise, and he's hoping that by warning her of Jenny's imminent arrival she'll keep clear. He's worried that Alice hasn't answered his texts or his calls. He feels frustrated, on edge, and he's wondering how he's going to get through these few days with Jenny without explaining and then facing the inevitable questions.

'Are you kidding? After that journey, I need a serious drink. I know you've had George and Helen here so I brought some supplies.'

'Don't worry. So did they, so I'm well stocked up. So what's the plan?'

'You sound like Helen,' she observes, taking the glass he pushes across the table towards her and raising it. 'I never have a plan when I come down here. That's the whole point of coming. Are you OK?'

'Yes, of course,' he answers quickly, lifting his glass to her. 'It's just been a bit busy, that's all.'

123

Jenny raises her eyebrows and he curses silently: now she'll want the details.

'Busy? In what way?'

'Well, you know. George and Helen staying.' He hesitates and then decides to sacrifice Em to her curiosity, just as he sacrificed her to distract George and Helen from Alice. 'And Bethany's best friend's staying in Dartmouth. Do you know her? Emily something. Em. She's all on her own and Bethany asked me to, you know, be friendly.'

Jenny's cool grey eyes appraise him and he feels foolish and irritable.

'How very . . . ' She hesitates over the word. ' . . . chivalrous of you. Yes, I've met Em.'

'Right. Well. I mentioned that you were coming down and she's suggested that we all have coffee on Friday morning.'

He's annoyed with himself for blurting it out so quickly after her arrival and takes a quick drink to steady himself. His life seems to be one chaotic muddle and he wishes that everyone would go away and leave him alone.

'Really?' Jenny is staring at him in surprise. 'Em seriously suggested that we should all have coffee together? I wonder why. Where?'

'In Dartmouth, at the place she likes to go to. Bayards Cove Café. I suppose she thought it would be a friendly thing to do. Perhaps Bethany's right and she gets a bit lonely down here on her own.'

'Then perhaps she should go back to London and all her friends,' suggests Jenny briskly. 'So do you want to do this, Leo?'

'I really don't mind,' he answers wretchedly. 'I think I did just mention that we might meet but if you can't bear the thought of it — '

'No, no,' she interrupts. 'If George and Helen can cope I'm sure I can. It's the polite thing to do, since she's invited us.'

Leo nods, relieved, then frowns. 'How did you know that George and Helen met her?' he asks.

'You said so just now,' Jenny answers quickly. 'Honestly, Leo, you do look a bit stressed. Are you sure you're OK?'

'Yes,' he says. 'Yes, of course I am.'

'Good,' she says cheerfully. 'Look, I'm going to take my things up, then we'll plan supper. I brought a few goodies with me. Don't finish all the wine. I'm in my usual room?'

'Yes, of course,' he says, pushing back his chair, as if to help her, but she shakes her head, smiling at him, and hurries away.

Leo takes a deep breath and another gulp of wine, then he fishes in his pocket for his phone and checks the messages. Nothing from Alice. He hesitates and then, deciding to take Jenny at her word, he sends a message to Em confirming coffee on Friday morning.

★　★　★

Upstairs, Jenny drops her bag on the bed and walks to the window. The room looks up the garden towards the arboretum and to the farmland beyond. No sweeping views of the sea here, but she likes its simplicity: the single bed, the small pine wardrobe and chest of drawers. After years of teaching, of classrooms and staff-rooms, she appreciates silence.

As she unpacks she analyses Leo's reactions and behaviour. He is certainly preoccupied, slightly on

125

edge, but there might be other reasons for that. To be distracted doesn't necessarily mean that you're in love. Now that she's seeing him in this new light she's rather taken aback by how attractive he still is and can well imagine that Em could have fallen for him. Leo's calm, self-contained charm might very well appeal to someone as volatile as Em, and it's possible that Leo might be flattered by her attention.

As she hangs up her shirts, throws her pyjamas on the bed, Jenny wonders how she should approach the forthcoming meeting. Should she be proprietorial, assuming that she and Leo naturally regard Em as they might one of their own children? That would be quite reasonable. But, on reflection, Jenny decides that she will wait; she'll play it by ear. She's rather surprised by how much she doesn't want Leo to be in love with Em. And it's not just for the sake of her sons' inheritance, it's because she doesn't want Leo to be hurt. This genuine anxiety takes her slightly by surprise, reminds her of how fond of him she is. Jenny finishes her unpacking and goes back downstairs to join him.

★   ★   ★

Em reads the text with delight. She feels as if she has won a minor victory, making Jenny come here rather than Em trekking over to Long Orchard and feeling slightly at a disadvantage on Jenny's territory. Em wonders how Leo will behave with his ex-wife present. Except that Jenny isn't an ex-wife. Bethany has explained their unusual relationship: still married but living separately, each staying in the other's house, very happy with the children and grandchildren.

'Sounds a bit weird,' Em said. 'Doesn't James think so?'

Bethany shook her head. 'He says they're used to it. Jenny was always dashing back to London. Just quick visits when they were young and then longer as they got older.'

Em made a face. 'Perhaps she's got a lover.'

Bethany burst out laughing. 'Jenny? Are you kidding me? She'd freeze the balls off him. I think that's why Leo doesn't mind her going. Well, you've met her.'

Remembering, Em wonders how Jenny will approach her. She might not want Leo but that doesn't mean she'll sit back and watch somebody else muscle in on her pitch. She thinks about Leo, wondering if he's had lovers. She suspects that the woman would have had to make the running. He's so self-contained that it's impossible to imagine him making a pass, chancing his arm. Yet he has that dry, quick sense of humour and when he smiles he's really rather gorgeous. And he's been so kind to her, asking her over, bringing his sister and her husband to meet her — and now his ex-wife . . . OK, wife. Em is aware that the elderly gentleman is leaving, raising his folded-up newspaper to her and she smiles at him.

'I hope you're communing with your muse,' he says, 'and not just day-dreaming. You won't get the word-count up that way, you know.'

She laughs in response and only afterwards thinks that it's an odd thing for him to say. What would he know about word-counts? But she opens the file and stares at the work in progress and sighs: if only it were.

★　★　★

127

When Tessa gives a little knock at the door, calls 'Hi,' and walks in, she's taken aback to see Jenny sitting at the kitchen table.

'Hi,' she says again, less certainly. 'I'm so sorry to barge in like that. I didn't know you were here.'

Jenny raises her eyebrows — she doesn't get up — and asks, 'Why would you?'

Tessa can think of no reasonable answer to this so she simply smiles and feels uncomfortable. Jenny makes no move to welcome her or ask the reason for her visit, she merely continues to look at her, eyebrows still raised, head very slightly at an angle, as if waiting for an answer. Tessa thinks how she would have hated to be one of her pupils, but she refuses to be coerced into some kind of explanation.

'Just dropped by on the way to the beach,' she says airily, 'but if Leo isn't around I'll leave you in peace.'

'He had to go down to the shop,' says Jenny, and frowns slightly as if irritated by giving away the information.

'Fine,' says Tessa swiftly. 'I might see him on his way back.'

She knows that Jenny is cross for making a false move. Now the meeting will take place without her there and she won't know why Tessa is walking into the kitchen in such a familiar way.

'You could stay,' she begins, but Tessa is too quick for her.

'Not a problem,' she answers. 'I've got Bodger outside, but thanks.'

She hurries away and down the lane, but there's no sign of Leo there or in the little square. Followed by Bodger, she walks out to the sea wall beside the steps and sees Leo almost immediately. He's

128

standing below her on the beach, head bent, looking at his phone. There's something in his stance, in his intensity, that prevents Tessa from simply calling to him. She remembers his expression when she was talking about someone reappearing from the past, his quick understanding when she told him about Sebastian, and she wonders how she might help him.

Instead of going down the stone steps, she walks along to the other end of the wall and out on to the beach so it looks as if she and Bodger are just coming back from a walk. She approaches slowly but Leo is already pushing his phone into his pocket, turning and climbing the steps. Disappointed, she quickens her pace but he's already at the top of the steps and heading off home.

$$\star \quad \star \quad \star$$

Leo walks quickly, hurrying back to Long Orchard. He invented the errand to the shop simply to have a few minutes to himself, to check his phone and to avoid Jenny's subtle interrogation. It's clear that she's noticed that he's slightly on edge and he can think of no way of putting her off the scent. It's not in his nature to dissimulate and he has no intention of mentioning Alice. When he gets in, however, it seems another complication has arisen.

'You've had a visitor,' Jenny says.

He wonders, irritably, why almost all Jenny's comments are thinly veiled challenges and then is seized by a sudden horror that it might have been Alice, turning up unexpectedly.

'A visitor?'

She raises her eyebrows. 'Yes. The woman who lives

with the two oldies in the cove. They invited us for tea once.'

'Tessa.' He's unable to hide his relief and Jenny stares at him, frowning a little.

'Yes,' she says. 'Tessa. She seemed very much at home. Just walked in unannounced and asked where you were. I hadn't realized you were so friendly.'

Leo knows a brief moment of overwhelming frustration and understands how someone might just be driven to an act of violence.

'I'm not sure how you're defining 'friendly',' he answers coolly. 'I've known Bea and Will and Tessa for at least fifteen years. How long do you need to know someone before they're allowed to drop in without a formal announcement?'

Jenny makes a little face. 'Have I touched a nerve? She wouldn't stay but said she might see you on her walk.'

She's clearly waiting for him to tell her if this happened and he shakes his head.

'No,' he says. 'No, I didn't see her.'

He wishes he had. It would have been very pleasant to spend a few minutes in Tessa's friendly, uncomplicated company. He searches around for a distraction, aware of Jenny's scrutiny.

'I couldn't get what I wanted at the shop,' he says. 'I thought I might dash into Kingsbridge. Want to come along for the ride?'

'Good idea,' she says. 'I need a few things and we could have lunch somewhere. I'll go and get my bag.'

He watches her go out, wonders how long he can keep this up and remembers again the verse his mother used to recite to them when they were children.

O what a tangled web we weave,
When first we practise to deceive!

Jenny goes to the loo, checks her hair in the mirror, and reaches for her bag. She's very glad now that she made the journey to Devon. She's never seen pragmatic, self-contained Leo so edgy and she's beginning to feel quite anxious. She wonders if Bethany is right to be worried about Em — and now there's Tessa, walking in so calmly and confidently and clearly expecting a warm welcome. Leo is an attractive man but both these girls are young enough to be his daughters and she can't imagine that there could be any serious danger.

Of course, Em is capable of imagining herself in love with him but Jenny still can't believe that Leo would seriously consider attaching himself to someone so volatile and foolish. As for Tessa . . . Jenny tries to remember what she knows about Tessa, which isn't much, except that she lives with the oldies and that she's married — or was. Perhaps there is something Leo isn't telling her; perhaps he's ill. Her heart gives a little clutch of fear. He always looks so fit, so tough. And, anyway, surely he would tell her. She and the boys would need to know if he had health problems. She needs to ask him, to be up front with it, and luckily she's never had a problem with confronting people.

Jenny checks her bag and goes downstairs to find Leo.

15

'She's gone rushing off again with Bodger,' Will says to Bea. 'If she's not haring off to Dartmouth she's dragging the poor old thing out for another walk. He's exhausted, poor chap.'

'But you don't think she's conceived a sudden passion for Leo?' asks Bea.

'Do *you*?' demands Will. 'Do you actually see dear old Leo in the role of lover to a girl young enough to be his daughter?'

'No,' admits Bea rather reluctantly, 'but men can be very foolish. And so can women,' she adds quickly, remembering her unsuitable and unrequited love for Tony Priest. 'It can be very painful. And you must admit that when Leo came over for that game of chess he was definitely distrait.'

'Yes, he was,' agrees Will snappishly, 'and if you'd left us alone for a moment I might just have got it out of him.'

Bea stares at him. 'Is this a quarrel?' she asks brightly.

Will closes his eyes for a moment and Bea can see that he's deciding whether to be long-suffering or to burst out laughing. Fortunately, he laughs.

'No,' he says, 'but with you popping in and out, offering him refreshments at odd moments, I didn't have a chance to get anything out of him.'

'My dear Will,' says Bea sceptically, 'do you really think that was going to happen? Leo's the last person to tell you his secrets, and especially not across the chessboard.'

'Why not?' demands Will. 'Because he likes to win,' answers Bea. 'And that's not at all an atmosphere in which to be confidential.' Will sighs. 'So what do we do? Tessa's still on some wonderful cloud nine, which I find disturbing.'

'I suppose,' says Bea thoughtfully, 'that she might just have confided in Leo, which would explain all those walks down the lane, and it would be very embarrassing for him when he sees us.'

'Perhaps we should just ask him outright,' suggests Will. 'Explain to him how worried we are about her.' 'I've got a better idea,' says Bea. 'I suggest that the next time she goes to Dartmouth we follow her.'

Will stares at her in awed amazement.

'Are you serious?'

Bea nods. 'Tessa is vulnerable just at the moment. It's been a real blow to her to leave the cove, and since Henry and now Charlotte are gone, she's very lonely. I know she's used to Giles being away but this is the first time that she's been really alone, and in a new home. She's been knocked off balance by something, or someone, and she needs a bit of protection.'

'I know you have your methods, Sherlock,' Will says, 'but would it really be that simple?'

'We don't know without trying, but yesterday, when I suggested an outing on Friday morning, she came over all self-conscious and said she didn't think she could.'

'And you really think she wouldn't notice us driving along behind her?'

'Don't be foolish,' says Bea sharply. 'I meant that we follow her once she's in the town. Naturally we go in early and park and then hope we see her. Dartmouth is a very small town and it shouldn't be too difficult to check the coffee shops.'

There's a silence, then: 'I can't believe we're having this conversation,' says Will.

'I know,' agrees Bea, 'and it probably won't work. It's a chance in a thousand but it's worth a try.'

'And suppose we find her with a man? What do we do? Do I march up to the table and tell him to come outside?'

'This is not a game,' says Bea severely. 'We shall have to decide that if we actually do find her with any-one. And I'm really hoping that we don't.'

Will looks serious. 'No, it's not a game. But I can't decide whether your plan is madness or genius, though there's not much difference between those two.'

Bea looks at him, her expression softening a lit-tle. 'Have you ever been in love, Will? I mean, really madly, crazily in love?'

He looks surprised and then thoughtful. 'Yes,' he says. 'I've know the 'pleasing plague', if that's what you mean, and bloody painful it is, too.'

'Tessa loves Giles and her children,' says Bea firmly, 'and I'm not prepared to stand by and watch it all be destroyed for some midsummer madness. So what about it?'

'You're on, Sherlock,' says Will. 'Tomorrow morn-ing it is.'

★ ★ ★

Bethany sits staring at another text from Em. She's being inundated with them and is beginning to feel very stressed. It sounds as if Em has really worked herself up into a passion for Leo and is intending to

134

make a play for him. It seems that she's really looking forward to this meeting in the coffee shop with
Leo and Jenny, and plans to make quite a big deal
about it. Bethany's seen Em like this before, knows
how crazy she can be, and now she's really worried.
It never occurred to her for a moment that Em might
be attracted to Leo — who is, let's face it, old enough
to be her father — and Bethany is beginning to feel
anxious that even Jenny might not be able to handle this. In fact, she might make it worse. She's quite
capable of being rude enough to Em to put Leo in
an embarrassing situation that might require him to
come over all chivalrous and that could be disastrous.
There needs to be a distraction — but what? She and
James were down at Long Orchard only a couple of
weekends ago so it would look odd if they suddenly
turned up, but on the other hand . . .

Bethany picks up her phone and makes a call.

16

On Friday morning Leo is beginning to feel nervous. He's been having a mild version of the third degree from Jenny about Em: why she's here, how long she's staying, what he thinks about her. He wonders why he was so crazy as to suggest this meeting but knows that it's to prevent Jenny suspecting he's got something on his mind. He can't help thinking about Alice, wondering where she is, if she'll turn up, and he knows that Jenny knows him far too well not to notice that he's not behaving in his usual manner.

I'm not cut out for this, he thinks. How can people live a double life? How do they manage the deceiving and the quick thinking?

They're standing together in the kitchen, preparing to leave for Dartmouth, when a message pings in. Leo seizes his phone from the kitchen table so quickly that Jenny stares at him in surprise.

'Expecting a call?' she asks sarcastically.

He tries to laugh it off. 'Just wondering if it's Em cancelling.'

But it isn't from Em, it's from Bethany.

Hi, Grando. James and I just had a great idea. It would be so much fun for the kids to see you and Granny together and we're thinking we might just dash down over the weekend. Could you cope? Bethany xx

'Well?' Jenny is still waiting.

'It's from Bethany,' he answers rather grimly, repressing an urge to swear loudly and throw things.

136

'She says our grandchildren would love to see us both together and she and James think they'll come down over the weekend.'

'How extraordinary of her,' says Jenny coolly. 'They saw us both together at Christmas in London when we all went to that ridiculous pantomime.'

'So what shall I reply?' he asks, his phone at the ready. 'I think your reaction might sound just a tad churlish.'

Jenny is considering, and he sees her frown change to a different expression: something has occurred to her and now she looks almost amused. Leo watches her with suspicion mixed with anxiety.

'What?' he says. 'Shall I just tactfully put them off?'

'No,' says Jenny. 'No, let them come, if you can cope with them again so quickly. I'd quite like to have a talk with Bethany.'

'Right,' he says. 'Sure? OK.'

He taps out a message and picks up his car keys. 'Shall we go?'

* * *

Em arrives at the café early. She won't be able to use her favourite table this morning, but there's a bigger one, also in the alcove. She decides that she'll order her usual mocha — she's got plenty of time before they arrive — and settles down to wait, full of excitement. She's really charged up for this, looking forward to a possible battle of wills with Jenny, spiced by the things she knows Jenny said about her to Bethany. At the same time she doesn't want to make Leo uncomfortable, especially if this is his way of making her feel like one of the family. His sister and her husband were

137

really nice and she knows she mustn't rock any boats, but at the same time she's not going to be treated like a child by Jenny. She opens her phone — she's left her laptop at home this morning — and begins to message Bethany.

Totally crazy. Sitting here waiting for Leo and Jenny. How weird is that? Definitely beginning to feel like a member of the family. The town is all geared up for the Bank Holiday weekend and is full of families on half-term. I love feeling a part of it all rather than just a visitor. I'd like to stay here for ever. E x

She presses Send and looks around her, smiling with satisfaction, ready for action. The old boy is coming in with his newspaper, smiling at her, ordering his Americano. The pretty woman has just come in, going to her usual table. Em feels confident, here on her own ground, looking forward to seeing Leo and ready to face Jenny. And here they are, opening the door, looking around for her. She puts on a smiling, happy face, except that Leo has stopped and is talking to the pretty woman, and now Jenny is joining in, which has rather spoiled the first moment. Still, Em manages to hold her smile and they are joining her at the table. There is the usual awkward moment as they greet, not quite knowing whether to give a hug or a little kiss on the cheek and she's slightly disappointed that Leo makes no attempt at any kind of embrace but looks around, getting his bearings. Before Em can speak, Jenny has sent Leo off to the bar with their order and is now looking at her with a kind of odd expression: wary, amused and totally in command of the situation.

Em's heart sinks a little. Somehow the sense that

she is in control, on her own territory, already knowing Leo, has begun to slip under that cool look.

'How nice to see you again, Em,' says Jenny insincerely. 'How odd that we should meet here. But of course you're staying in Bethany's family's bolt hole, aren't you? Great news, by the way. Bethany and James and the boys are coming down again tomorrow. Or did you know? So odd that they should be coming again so soon. You must come over.'

She turns as Leo comes back to the table, putting his wallet away. He looks harassed, not at all lover-like, and Em's heart sinks still further.

'I was just telling Emily that Bethany et al. will be down tomorrow and that she must come over and see them. They might like to go to the beach or out on the cliffs.'

Having classed Em with their children, Jenny smiles at Leo, who nods.

'Of course,' he agrees. 'Good idea. So how's the work coming on, Em?'

She tries to seize this as evidence of their previous intimacy, but there's very little to work on, and Jenny's grey-eyed gaze seems to freeze her brain. She's relieved when the coffee arrives and she can take a moment to sit back and regain her composure.

★ ★ ★

'I can't do it,' says Will. 'It seemed different back at home last evening, like a sort of game that Henry might devise. But now it's real. This is Tessa we're talking about and I can't follow her about and spy on her.'

'I know,' says Bea. 'Now we're here I feel the same.

139

I think I was a bit overwrought yesterday. It's just that I can't bear to see anything go wrong with them.'

They stand together in the sunshine, beside the boat float, and then Will takes her arm and presses it.

'Me, too. But this isn't the way. Come on. Let's go and have coffee in the Castle.'

They go in together, choose a table, order coffee. Each of them is at a loss as to how to proceed.

'I suppose,' says Will at last, 'that really it's none of our business.'

'But it's Tessa and Giles we're talking about,' protests Bea. 'Not forgetting Henry and Charlotte.'

She nearly adds 'and Bodger,' but realizes how foolish that sounds.

'Even so,' says Will, 'I suspect that we could do far more harm than good if we're not careful. That's the trouble with loving people: you can get things out of perspective.'

'I suppose so,' says Bea reluctantly. 'I wish Giles would come home.'

'They'll all be home soon,' Will says comfortingly. 'Henry and Charlotte will be back from uni, and Giles hasn't got much longer on this assignment, as far as I can remember. I expect it will sort itself out. Something will happen, you'll see.'

★ ★ ★

As soon as she is able, Tessa slips out of the café. The surprise of seeing Leo, of trying to talk to him easily and naturally, was like a shock wave through her brain, startling her back into reality. What if Sebastian had already arrived and they'd been sitting together, laughing and intimate, as they have been before? No

140

doubt Leo would have guessed that this was the revenant she spoke of, but to be taken unawares, to be exposed, would have been humiliating.

Hurrying out into the street, she feels ashamed, and when she sees Sebastian coming towards her, his face lighting with a smile, she feels utterly confused. He sees at once that something is wrong and looks concerned.

'A friend,' she says, breathlessly. 'A friend came in and I thought it might look a bit, well, you know.'

The very fact that she's saying these words make her feel even more ashamed, and she takes his arm, turning him away from the cove.

'Let's go to the Royal Castle,' she says.

'And do none of your friends go to the Castle?' he asks lightly, trying to joke her out of her anxiety. 'And, anyway, why shouldn't two old friends meet for coffee?'

She drops his arm but doesn't answer: she knows that they haven't been behaving like two old friends having coffee. There's a risk that she might see someone she knows — of course there always has been — but at least Bea and Will are in Kingsbridge so she should be fairly safe. Nevertheless, the sense of crazy happiness, the effervescence, has vanished, blown away in that cold breath of reality and, as if he senses it, Sebastian puts his arm around her shoulders, holding her lightly but firmly against him.

★ ★ ★

The elderly man finishes the crossword and glances around. As he folds his newspaper and stands up he wonders why the blonde woman left so abruptly.

141

There's another woman here again today with a tired but pretty face, wearing a silk scarf tied loosely over her head. He can guess the reason for the scarf. His wife used to wear one like that after the chemo; said it was less itchy than the wig. It was after she died, fifteen years ago, that he started to write the detective fiction for which he is so well known. He's glad, though, that few people recognize writers and he is allowed to move about mostly unrecognized. He puts his paper under his arm and goes out.

* * *

Alice sits in the furthest corner, watching. Her heart almost stops beating when Leo walks in, and instinctively she raises her mug of hot chocolate to her lips with both hands as if to hide her face. After such a long time, with the scarf tied loosely so it partly obscures her face, she doesn't really believe that Leo will recognize her, but she's taking no chances and she's glad that he stops to talk to a woman near the bar, which distracts him. She's guessing that the smart, grey-haired woman is his wife — she looks just a little like Helen — and she studies her with interest. She's meeting someone already here, sitting in the alcove, probably the girl who was looking at her phone, and now Alice can no longer see them properly.

She wonders if she should slip out. She's spent the last two nights in the room for rent upstairs but other people have booked from today and Alice knows she must go back to Torcross. It was foolish to run away, she realizes that now, but she must meet Leo alone for the first time after all these years, not amongst his family.

Without Jason, with Adam gone to New York, she feels untethered again, and she hopes that Leo might keep her grounded for the few months she has left to her. It's so good to be back here where she always felt so much at home, but she needs Leo to make the final gesture of welcome.

★　★　★

Sebastian has never felt so uncomfortable. He and Tessa walk into the bar of the Royal Castle, glance around for a table, and he sees two old dears staring at him as if he's the villain in a pantomime. Beside him, Tessa gives a little gasp of shock, but before she can speak, the old guy is getting up, smiling at them, as if he's actually expecting him and Tessa to join them. Which they do.

Sebastian realizes that these are the two that Tessa speaks about, Bea and Will, and he's obliged to be pleasant while Tessa is saying: 'Look who I met in the town. You remember Sebastian? His boy's at the College and he's been visiting him.'

She hurries away to buy coffee whilst the old boy beams and the old girl gives him a quick grilling: how long is he here, where does he live?

After a while, aware of Tessa sitting stiff and cool beside him, Sebastian begins to fear that this is going to be over before it's begun. It was always going to be difficult with Tessa, but with these two watching over her he suspects that he doesn't stand a chance.

Cursing under his breath, Sebastian finishes his coffee, glances at his watch, smiles at them all and says he must go; that it was great to meet them again, that he'll be in touch. Outside he hangs about, hoping that Tessa might be able to get away and follow him out, but the moments pass and there is no sign of her. Still cursing, he goes to find his car, climbs in and drives away.

★ ★ ★

'Well, if it weren't for poor Tessa's pride, I'd say that was almost an answer to a prayer,' says Will.

After Sebastian left they all sat for a while, finishing coffee, talking as if nothing out of the ordinary had happened. Now Tessa has gone upstairs to the loo and Bea and Will sit for a moment in silence.

'It was such a shock, her walking in like that, I almost believed she'd guessed what we were planning to do,' says Bea at last. 'But in a way it was just as we hoped. And in an odd way, I think she was almost pleased to see us. Relieved, if you know what I mean. Maybe that's all she needed to wake her up.'

'Poor Tessa,' says Will. 'A rather rude awakening from whatever dream she was having.'

'Yes,' says Bea, thinking of her own foolish passion for Tony Priest. She shakes her head sadly. "Lord, what fools these mortals be!"

Will watches her thoughtfully, glances at his watch. 'Let's have a drink and then perhaps some lunch. I'm sure Tessa will join us.'

'Good idea,' Bea answers gratefully. 'I'll have a gin and tonic.'

★ ★ ★

Starry, starry night. The stars dazzle in the darkness and Leo is drawn down to the beach, to stare across

144

the black and silver sea to the horizon where a luminous glow heralds the moonrise. He sits down on the still-warm stones, his arms folded round his knees, thankful that the weekend is over and everyone has gone. It's been rather a nightmare few days and the Saturday morning that Em came over was the worst of all. It was as if he were present at a play in which he was obliged to take part but hadn't been given a script or stage directions. He could see that Jenny and Bethany were slightly at odds, and that Em was in some heightened state of excitement, and in the end he'd simply got hold of James and the boys and gone up on the cliffs to walk to Start Point. When they got back, Em had gone, Bethany seemed to be sulking, and Jenny was in one of her sarcastic moods. To his relief, everyone decided to leave on Sunday afternoon, in an effort, they all said, to beat the Bank Holiday Monday traffic. And so here he is, alone again.

Listening to the shush of the restless waves, Leo gives himself up to the past. He remembers that other starry night as he and Alice lay side by side, her thin fingers clutching his, her voice whispering to him, 'We'll always be together, won't we, old Lion?'

How quickly and easily he'd given his promise: but at nearly thirteen, promises come easily, everything is possible. Now he sits, hugging his knees, willing her to appear beside him.

From her balcony above, Alice watches him. He sent her another text earlier this afternoon.

Everyone has gone. Please come home. L x

And she replied:

I will. X

She wonders if he, too, is remembering that other starry, starry night when they lay together on the

145

beach and, without giving herself chance to think, she goes quickly down the stairs and out on to the shingle. She walks quietly, approaching him from behind, and when he turns quickly, staring up at her, she stops, waiting.

Leo gazes at her. He can hardly believe it. In the starry darkness it's as if Alice has come back from the past. In her long skirt, with her hair in a plait, she seems unchanged, and he gets up on to his knees and holds out his hands to her. Only when she comes close to him does he see that she has aged and, as she kneels beside him and raises her hands to remove the wig, he understands her reticence, her fear, and he is filled with compassion and love. Slowly he raises his own hands and lays them tenderly, gently, on the fragile skull, and she bends her head, almost weeping with relief as she nestles against him.

He holds her close and kisses her. 'Welcome home, Al,' he says.

INTERLUDE

The long June days are unpredictable: high winds, sudden downpours, hot sunshine. Each day is a gift to Leo and Alice: precious hours spent in reminiscence, in companionship and discovery. When Alice finally comes home to Long Orchard she stands silent, as if she has entered another world, one that she left more than forty years ago, and she can hardly absorb it. Leo waits, apprehensively, watching her, not quite knowing how this scene should be played. The prodigal son was greeted with music and dancing, and the killing of livestock, but Leo is fairly confident that none of these things would be appropriate. And anyway, Alice doesn't quite fit into that role. This homecoming is an odd one and he needs her to take the lead. In true Alice style she's played down the whole aspect of her illness and its treatment, and he senses that what is needed here is positivity, a sense of holiday, life-affirming reconnection. To begin with he was anxious at the prospect and his default mode of checking with someone — Helen, Jenny — on what might be needed in this situation threatened to overcome his natural instincts. But very quickly he decided to trust himself, to allow Alice to guide this reunion.

'This is so strange,' she says, as he leads her into the house. 'Everything is the same, but different.'

She walks about, touching things — 'You've still got the Peter Rabbit mug. I don't believe it' — peering from the window, as if she is acclimatizing herself. And still Leo watches her, waiting to anticipate some need, longing for her to relax. Something is required to mark the occasion, a gesture to begin this new chapter, but he can't quite decide what it should be. Offering to bring her bags in from her car, to show her upstairs to her room, doesn't quite cut it, somehow. Less than twenty-four hours have passed since their emotional reunion on the beach and now that she's here he's momentarily at a loss. Unexpectedly, his mother's advice carries him through: 'In moments of joy or despair there's nothing like a glass of fizz.' He doesn't have champagne but he knows there is a bottle of prosecco kept for moments such as these with his family, and now he goes into the larder and takes it down from the shelf.

Alice has wandered through to the study, looking along the bookshelves, and he follows her, the bottle in his hand.

'Could you manage some of this?' he asks, holding it up. 'Seems rather appropriate for a homecoming.'

She turns to look, and gives a laugh of delight.

'That's just perfect,' she says. 'You know, I've imagined this so many times and now I can't believe it's happening. I know it's crazy . . .'

She pauses, and he can see that suddenly she's near to tears.

'It's fine,' he assures her quickly. 'Just take your time to readjust.'

She follows him back into the kitchen, watches while he opens the bottle and pours the wine, and takes her glass. He can sense her emotions swinging between joy at being back and sadness of all that has been missed, and he decides that he must remain prosaic.

'Everyone has gone,' he says, 'so it's rather as if a

swarm of locusts has passed through. I haven't had time to go shopping so I suggest we walk down to the pub for supper. Are you OK with that?'

'Sounds fine,' she says, sipping her wine. 'Sorry, I'm all over the place. It's just so weird that I'm standing here, in this kitchen, drinking prosecco with you.'

'We've got a lot of catching up to do,' he agrees. 'You're in your old room, so no change there.'

She's taken a photograph from the dresser and studies it intently.

'My son, James,' says Leo, 'with his son, Josh. Josh is three.'

She sets it back on the shelf and turns, smiling at him. 'I've brought some photographs with me. You might have a bit of a shock when you see my Adam.'

Leo guesses at her meaning, and hesitates. 'Is that why you never came back?'

'I couldn't risk it,' she says sadly. 'After all, what was there to gain from it? My old dad used to keep me informed from time to time, tell me how happy you all were. How could I have come back alone? Imagine all the questions.' She shakes her head. 'It was better to let sleeping dogs lie, but so hard not to be able to tell you why.'

He holds his glass up. 'That was then and this is now.'

She nods but her face is anxious. 'But you'll tell Helen that I'm here?'

'Yes, I'll tell Helen that you're here and we'll play it as it comes. Did I tell you that Mags and John are living in Edinburgh? I doubt they'll be down but I'm pretty sure Helen and George will come. I know Helen is a bit of a one for the third degree, but given that you've been through a very tough time recently

149

I doubt you'll have much trouble. Anyway, we'll cope with it. Don't let it spoil our time together.'

'No, I won't. And I'd so much like to see them and somehow make things right as far as I can, though I'm not looking forward to it. Helen's bound to ask questions. Am I married? Children? Grandchildren? I still don't know how I'm going to handle it.'

'One step at a time,' Leo says cheerfully. 'Let's go and have some supper before the pub gets too full, and then we'll get you settled in.'

★   ★   ★

So it begins, this period of unexpected happiness. Each morning as she stands at the bedroom window, looking to see what weather the day will bring, wondering what rediscovery from the past might be revealed, Alice gives thanks that she has been brave enough to return. In her heart she knows that she has come seeking confirmation that she really exists; that she is still somehow tethered to this planet. Back then, after her mother died, in that mad round of army bases, boarding schools and kind relatives, it was only here at Long Orchard that she felt secure. Leo and his sisters and her uncle and aunt were her family: she belonged. How strange it is to come back, to find Leo still here, so much unchanged: the paintings on the walls, pieces of china, the old oak table in the kitchen. As she dresses, folds the soft scarf around her head, Alice refuses to allow herself to think about the day when she will leave again. It cannot be acknowledged yet, lest it should corrode the present happiness.

Leo is an easy companion, prepared to enter into each new plan, ready to listen when she needs to speak. She is delighted with what he has achieved in the garden. The wildflower meadow is past its best but easy to imagine in all its glory; the arboretum is beautifully designed, full of shape and colour.

'Jason would have loved this,' she exclaimed, gazing round in delight when they toured the garden. 'You should build a summer house in the meadow so you can sit and look at all this. If you put it at the top you'll be able to see way beyond to the sea.'

As she descends the stairs and passes through the study she can hear voices in the kitchen: Leo's voice and the voice of a younger man. She hesitates and then walks in. They both turn to look at her. The other voice belongs to a young man in his late teens or early twenties. He's tall, dark-haired, attractive. He smiles at her, a warm, wide smile, and she smiles back at him, guessing who he might be.

'This is Henry,' Leo is saying, confirming her guess. 'I told you about all the help he's given me in the garden. And I was just telling him about your idea for building some kind of shelter up in the meadow.'

'It's a great idea,' says Henry enthusiastically. 'I'm sure we could manage something as long as it's not too big or then you might need planning permission.'

'Good thinking, Batman,' murmurs Leo, and Henry grins at him.

Alice warms to this young man, knowing that he's the son of one of Leo's little group of friends. She's already met Will briefly at Stokeley Farm Shop but she has yet to meet Henry's parents, and Bea. Leo has explained to her that Giles and Tessa are concerned about Henry's future, that he has no vocation for anything except a passion for the land. He's just back from university and will be working at Stokeley

151

during the holidays, quite contented.

Remembering this, and looking at him in his T-shirt and jeans, she is reminded of Jason when she first met him. It was easier back then to step out of the mainstream, to be a little different. They'd been lucky to be employed by the hill farmer, to live simply and happily, during those early years together. Now, their little cottage would be a holiday home, and health and safety would have banned a lot of the jobs that Jason had so readily undertaken.

'I'm thinking,' Leo is saying, 'that we should crack on with this project. Get it done while Alice is with us.'

'Just something simple,' she says, entering into the spirit of the venture. 'Not anything pretentious. It needs to be in keeping with its surroundings.'

Henry takes out his phone. 'I'll check a few things out and you can tell me if you like them.'

'Alice hasn't had breakfast yet,' says Leo. 'Sit down and do it while she's eating.'

'I can't,' answers Henry regretfully. 'I've got to get to work. That's why I'm early. Mum said to drop by to ask if you'd both like to come to supper with Wilby. Or lunch. Or something.'

Alice laughs. 'That's comprehensive,' she says. 'And who or what is Wilby?'

Leo grins. 'It's Henry's name for Will and Bea, Tessa's cousins, and so, by extension, Henry's.'

'OK,' says Alice. 'So which, in your view, would be the best of all of those options?'

'Supper,' answers Henry at once. 'Then I can be there. I might be working at lunchtime.'

'Supper it is, then,' agrees Alice. 'And please tell your mother I'm really looking forward to meeting her. And Wilby, of course.'

Henry nods, raises a hand in farewell, and disappears.

'You're honoured,' says Leo. 'Henry doesn't usually grace our little group with his presence.'

'He's rather gorgeous,' murmurs Alice. 'Or am I not allowed to say things like that in our politically correct age?'

Leo shrugs as he puts a bowl of fruit salad and some cereal on the table. 'Don't see why not. He's a good-looking boy. And a very nice one.'

'And is he like his mother? Or his father?'

'Oh, he's very like Giles,' says Leo. 'Temperamentally and physically.'

Alice raises her eyebrows and sits down at the table. 'Lucky old Tessa,' she says.

★　★　★

Henry strides away down the lane, his head busy with this new idea. He enjoys a project and is pleased to be enjoined in the building of the pavilion. His meeting with Alice has touched him. He already knows her story. Leo has warned them about the death of her partner, quickly followed by the diagnosis of cancer, the operation, and then chemo, which is why she sometimes wears a wig and sometimes a scarf. Leo said that Alice won't want to talk about any of it, that he wants this to be a happy time for his cousin, and they can all understand that.

It's hot in the lane and dog roses are flowering in the hedgerows. The farmer has seized these hot, dry few days to bring the hay in and Henry can hear the machine and smell the scent of new-cut grass. He's

153

glad Leo warned them about Alice otherwise he might have stared at the scarf swathed around her head. It looked unusual, almost theatrical, yet in a strange way it suited her. Oddly, it made her look much younger than she is, and he feels sad for all that she's gone through.

'How terrible it all is,' Mum sympathized, when she was telling him what Leo had said. 'Poor woman. First to lose her partner and then to have to deal with this bloody cancer all on her own. And not only that, her son's going through a divorce in New York.'

Now that he's met Alice, Henry thinks about all this in light of the proposed supper party.

'Subjects of conversation might be tricky,' Mum said thoughtfully. 'We'll have to be very tactful. But I know it means a lot to Leo so we'll just have to do our best. Will and Bea will help it along.'

And now there is something they can talk about, thinks Henry. The pavilion. Reasons to be cheerful. He pauses at the end of the lane, waiting for some cars to pass along the main road, then crosses it and heads up towards the farm.

★ ★ ★

Will and Bea are sitting in their little courtyard, amongst the tubs and planters full of flowers, enjoying the colour and the warmth. Tessa stands beside the small wicker table, making notes on her shopping list.

'OK,' she says. 'If you're sure that's everything. It's going to be hot so I'm dashing off now. Bodger's had a walk and I've left him in the utility-room with all the windows open.'

154

'We'll keep an eye,' says Will. 'So you haven't met Alice yet?'

He's feeling rather pleased that he got in first here, meeting Alice when he was shopping at the farm shop. Will knows it's childish but it's nice to be ahead of the game for a change. And he was very taken with Leo's cousin. There was a vivacity, a rather delightful ease in her friendly approach, that made him feel that they were old friends rather than new acquaintances. Leo invited him to join them for coffee and Will accepted very readily. Alice asked him about his life in Switzerland; told him how she'd been a chalet girl when she was very young, making them laugh. Will thoroughly enjoyed the encounter and is now very pleased that Tessa is inviting them all to a lunch or a supper.

'No,' answers Tessa, 'not yet. I've sent Henry over this morning with an invitation and then we'll get something sorted out. I'll let you know.' She smiles at him. 'It's clear she made a good impression on you.'

Bea rolls her eyes. 'Can't stop talking about her.'

'I think what struck me,' says Will, ignoring Bea's expression, 'is that she wasn't at all what I was expecting. After all, given what's happened to her in these last few years I was expecting someone rather sad, almost an invalid, I suppose, and yet she wasn't a bit like that.'

'Well, I'm very glad,' says Tessa. 'I'm feeling the least bit anxious about striking the right note. After all, she must be a little daunted about meeting us all. It's one reason I sent Henry over with the invitation. It was a chance for her to meet him, so that she'll feel she's among friends.'

'I wondered if you might drop in on them,' says Bea. 'I know you do that sometimes when you're walking

155

Bodger down the lane.'

'I have thought about it,' replies Tessa, frowning. 'It's just that I wondered if it might be rather . . . you know, difficult.'

Before Bea can reply, Will steps in. 'I can see that. But I think we're all probably being a bit too sensitive about the fact that Alice has been having so many problems. Sometimes people in her position are quite grateful to be treated normally rather than tiptoed round, or approached with long faces and special voices. Leo was quite right to warn us, but I don't think you need to worry, Tessa.'

'Well, that's comforting,' says Tessa. 'Thanks, Will. I must be off. See you later.'

They sit in silence, hear the car engine fire up and pull out, and then Bea looks at Will.

'Getting to be quite the philosopher in your old age,' she says. 'I can't wait to meet her.'

Will tilts back his head, raising his face to the sun, closes his eyes and smiles.

If you're not one up you're one down, he thinks. First move to me.

* * *

Tessa drives through the village, thinking about what Will has said. It strikes true and she determines to stop fussing about her party and approach it more light-heartedly. She wants it to be a success mainly for Leo because she knows how much this means to him, but there's always a danger of over-thinking things, and Will is right. In one's anxiety not to be insensitive it's easy to be almost morbidly sympathetic. She's looking forward to hearing what Henry has to say about Alice and, meanwhile, she intends to put it out of her head and simply enjoy this moment: the thrift growing along the foreshore and the gleam of water, windbreaks on the beach and the flash of white sails under the cliffs.

Tessa drives slowly along the quiet coastal road. Somehow, on a day like this, she simply can't feel responsible. It's one of those days for sitting with a glass of wine or a cup of coffee, watching the boats and the people and the world in general.

One of those perfect days when there's a car parking space just when you need it, your favourite table in your favourite café is empty and waiting for you, and your favourite person in all the world comes in and sits down next to you.

And who would that be? The thought jolts her out of her peacefulness. She glances in the mirror, puts her foot down and accelerates away towards Dartmouth.

★ ★ ★

Sometimes, just sometimes, as they walk, or drive, or sit with a glass of wine in a pub, Alice is able to live in the moment. Walking on the beach at Bigbury, feeling the sand between her toes and a precipitate wave curling round her ankles; standing at Combestone Tor in the shadow of the rocks and looking out across the sweep of the moor; strolling in the narrow streets of Salcombe and buying a pasty to eat, sitting on the quay and watching the boats in the sunshine. Living in these moments she is able to forget the shadow hovering close, to pretend that the inevitable future might never come.

The most difficult time was the visit from Helen and George. It was made worse by Leo being aware of her fears and anxious for her, so that she was obliged to be doubly strong. Together they checked some of the photos on Alice's phone. She knew that Helen would demand to see photos of the family and that it would be necessary to feed her curiosity.

'Maya's beautiful,' Leo says. 'She's so like you, Al. But, goodness, it's extraordinary how like his father Adam is. I can see why you could never have brought him back. But how hard for you. God, what a bloody mess it all was.'

She knows how much Leo reproaches himself for leaving her to fend for herself, and she's tried hard to show him that this was not his responsibility, but he finds it difficult to accept.

'I knew that Helen might never forgive him,' she said to Leo. 'And what would it have achieved? I didn't ever want to be with George and he was in love with Helen. I'm very fond of Helen and would have hated to hurt her because of one silly moment of weakness. But you mustn't think I don't feel guilty that George doesn't know he has a handsome, clever son and a beautiful granddaughter. I know he has a son and a daughter with Helen, and grandchildren, so I just feel grateful for that. And how might it have affected Adam? He adored Jason. I simply couldn't take the chance. But I think I must see George and Helen now that they know I'm here and they want to come down. I'm almost glad that Mags and John are too far away to make the journey. I don't think I'd cope with everyone. It's a good thing,' she added wryly, 'that I was so unreliable. Now here. Now there. Nobody ever quite knew where I was. And, after all, we only saw each other for those few weeks in the summer, didn't we? I shall simply have to bluff my way through it and Helen will think that I'm just as irresponsible as I always was.'

'You have to remember,' Leo said, 'that neither of them has any idea about Adam. They won't be expecting it or be looking for it. And after all, you were the one who carried the can. Don't be so hard on yourself.'

She could see that it hurt Leo to portray her like this, but it couldn't be helped and she braced herself for the ordeal. But, as so often is the case, it turned out to be less fearsome than she imagined.

Kind Helen was much too pleased to see her to be too judgemental. She reproved her little cousin, of course, and told her how much they all worried about her, but that was to be expected. Still, there was so much to catch up on and, with Leo's help, Alice was able to turn the conversation on to Helen's family. There was much to talk about here and it was clear that both George and Helen were aware both of Alice's illness and her bereavement, which made it rather uncomfortable for them to question her too closely about her past.

Taking Leo's advice, she wore her wig, her plait of ashy brown, which from a distance gave her a more youthful look. After one glance Helen kept her eyes away from it, but Alice could see George studying it when he thought she wasn't looking, and she wondered whether to make some light-hearted comment, but in the end decided not to. He was politely interested in the photos, but Helen commented on how pretty Maya was and how much like Alice when she was young, and that they hoped to meet her before too long. It was clear that Alice's situation overshadowed any suspicion or doubts in Helen's mind about George's attraction for her cousin — or at least put them into perspective — and her natural kindness and sympathy enabled the meeting to pass without any difficulties. And Bax was a wonderful addition to the party. He could be relied upon to smooth any awkward pause. His genial presence, always ready to be stroked or to be given a treat, carried everyone across any difficult moment.

Alice knew that Leo was right. Her fear was based on her secret knowledge, and George and Helen were simply happy to welcome her back into the fold.

'Nevertheless,' remarked Leo rather crossly afterwards, 'I still don't see why George should get away with it scot-free.'

But Alice was too relieved to argue or agree; she was simply glad that it was all over, that her secret was still safe and she could relax. Gladly she and Leo resumed their happy companionship.

Yet each morning it's all to do again. Those few brief seconds before the knowledge that something awful has happened twists in the gut, and then the full waking to reality. Here, with Leo, she is able to focus on the plans for the day ahead, trusting that his company will be enough to hold back the demons. And Henry, with his youth and enthusiasm, is another blessing. She likes to be with him, up in the meadow, watching him working, seeing the pavilion taking shape.

'I have a granddaughter just a little younger than you,' she told him. 'Her name is Maya.'

He was interested, asking questions, and she showed him several photographs she kept on her phone. He studied them approvingly but cautiously.

'She looks nice,' he said rather inadequately.

'Yes,' Alice agreed. 'She's very nice. Very determined, works hard, but she's fun, too.'

He went back to work and she watched him, wondering how he and Maya would get on together and hoping that maybe they might one day have the kind of friendship that she and Leo share. Soon Maya will have no family close at hand and it would be comforting to think that she might have Leo and Henry as friends, and a place of refuge here at Long Orchard.

But the days are passing quickly, and soon she must go back to her little cottage and prepare herself for what is coming. These few weeks will sustain her, give her courage, and once the pavilion is finished it will be time for her to leave, but this time the leaving will be different. She has a plan, and this plan gives her a sense of peace and even happiness.

PART TWO

PART TWO

17

Leo pays for his shopping, picks up the bag and his newspaper and carries them through to the café. He sits down with his back to the wooden plank partition that separates the farm shop from the café. From here he can gaze out through the glass doors, which take up the whole of the end wall, to the courtyard where people are sitting at wooden tables, with their dogs beside them, or looking at the plants for sale. If he looks up, the curved wooden ceiling suggests the inside of an old sailing boat, and all around him the grey walls are covered with paintings by local artists and notices of forthcoming events.

A slant of early autumn sunshine, spearing the mist, reflects off the high ceiling and lights up his table. This place has become a refuge for him in the last few weeks, since Alice died. Holding his paper, still folded, Leo stares across it unseeingly, his mind still locked into the happy time they had together: taking the sea tractor from Bigbury across to Burgh Island, cream teas at Blackpool Sands, walks on the beach and on the cliffs. All the while, as she talked and talked, and they laughed and reminisced, it hadn't occurred to him that these were her last days. He believed her when she told him she was in remission, that she was clear, and when she said that she must go home to make sure all was well, and then she was going to visit her family, but that one day soon she would be back again, he believed her. For the second time he allowed her to go, and turned his attention to the summer holidays and the invasions of his family.

Leo groans inwardly: the failures and humiliations of our pasts remain. How could he have been so blind, so foolish? Helen was delighted to see her, though clearly puzzled as to why such a lengthy silence was maintained. But forty years is a long time, easily glossed over, and their visit was brief. George, not knowing that he had a son, was able to play his part with grace and charm, and even sharp-eyed Helen seemed satisfied with his brotherly approach to the situation.

'But he must never meet Adam,' Alice said, after they'd gone.

She seemed changed, after the meeting, as if some huge effort of will carried her through it and then burned out, leaving her weak. In retrospect, Leo can make sense of it. Her return had been exactly that: a determination to do this one last thing.

'I suppose,' he answered her cautiously, 'that there's no real reason why he should. He knows you're here?'

She nodded, not looking at him. 'Though he doesn't really know where 'here' actually is. And, anyway, he's a bit distracted at the moment. I told you.'

Yes, he knew that Adam was in the middle of an acrimonious divorce, that he'd been playing away and his wife had left him. Their eighteen-year-old daughter, Maya, was studying in Italy and would be going to Cambridge this autumn to read Modern Languages. How Alice loved Maya. Looking at the photographs on Alice's phone, Leo could understand why.

'She's so like you were,' he said, studying the happy, laughing, slender girl. 'It's amazing. I'd love to meet her.'

'Maybe,' answered Alice, closing her phone. 'Maybe one day.'

Leo is aware of someone standing by his table and looks up startled, his reverie broken. Giles is watching him with a half-tentative, half-hopeful expression and Leo pulls himself together and gestures to the chair opposite.

'Are you going to join me?' he asks.

Now that he's begun this routine of stopping for coffee when he comes to Stokeley to shop, Leo has become used to seeing his friends: Bea and Will, Tessa, Giles. They know why he's here — Alice's death was a shock to them all but especially to him — and in different ways they show their concern for him.

Giles puts his bag of shopping on the floor, orders coffee and sits down.

'Thanks,' he says. 'I haven't seen you for a bit and I want to thank you for being so patient with Henry this summer. He's been driving us all mad and his sessions working with you seem to have given him a focus. And working here at Stokeley. He likes growing things but not much else. His time at uni may have been utterly pointless.'

Leo remembers how Alice had really liked Henry; she said he reminded her of Jason.

'If he'd had a son he'd have been like Henry,' she said rather wistfully, one evening after Henry had gone home after working up in the arboretum. 'He has that same tendency to nurture that Jason had. Oh God, I miss him.'

Leo knew that there were no adequate words of consolation, but simply gave silent thanks that she'd had Jason to keep her centred. He wished he could have met him.

'Henry's a good boy,' Leo says now, refocusing his attention. 'I think you're worrying too much.'

Giles nods. 'Yes, he can be very charming, but we still don't quite know in which direction to point him. Tessa's getting a bit wound up about it.'

He hesitates, stirring some sugar into his coffee, and Leo watches him sympathetically. Since his return he and Giles have had one or two conversations about Tessa. Nothing too personal, just that he's a bit worried about her, that she's behaving rather oddly.

'Not grumpy,' he said, 'or anything like that. The reverse. Rather like she thinks she needs to reassure me that everything's fine, which is a bit odd.'

Leo remained silent, unable to break Tessa's confidences, hating the situation and wondering why he had suddenly become everyone's go-to counsellor.

'Henry's a good lad,' he repeats. 'It's been fun having him around. And I've been thinking about what he might do.'

'Any suggestions gratefully received,' answers Giles, 'before I go completely round the bend. Living with an unemployed twenty-one-year-old would be hell on wheels.'

Leo grins sympathetically. 'I get that, but my suggestion might not solve that problem.'

Giles sighs. 'Let's have it anyway. Is there money in it?'

'There might be. I was wondering if he could apply for a job on the Sharpham Estate near Totnes. Vineyards, cheese-making, the café. It's an amazing place. They must need all sorts of people and it could lead on to other things. It might be worth a try just to focus him and get him started.'

Giles looks thoughtful. 'It's a thought. He's not afraid to graft, I'll say that for him. Thanks, Leo.' He hesitates. 'Do you know anyone there?'

Leo laughs. 'It just so happens that we did some work for them, yes. I could put in a word.'

'Thanks, mate. Though I never quite saw Henry as a gardener. I mean, a gardener? Will he be able to support himself?'

'Alan Titchmarsh?' murmurs Leo. 'Monty Don?'

'OK, but you know what I mean.'

Leo thinks of his own sons, in faceless offices in London, and reflects on the beauties of the Sharpham Estate down on the River Dart.

He shrugs. 'It worked for me.'

Giles looks embarrassed. 'But you were in land and estate management.'

'But Henry could do that. It would be interesting for him to see how a big estate works. Perhaps he should apply for one of the courses at Cirencester.'

Giles is interested. 'It's an idea. He's certainly loved working with you, this summer, and here at Stokeley.'

'I think it's what his heart wants,' agrees Leo. 'Shall I open up a line of communication, just to see how the land lies, if you'll excuse the pun?'

'I suppose I should just run it past Tessa,' says Giles cautiously. 'And Henry, of course.'

'Of course,' agrees Leo, 'but I don't want to get his hopes up. My enquiry would be very casual. No names, nothing to lose.'

'That would be great,' says Giles. 'Thanks.'

He glances past Leo and his expression changes to an odd mix of pride, apprehension and affection. Leo recognizes the face of a man who is looking at his child and smiles to himself.

'Hello, Henry,' he says without looking round.

'Hi,' says Henry, appearing beside him and beaming down at him. 'How did you know it was me?'

'My sixth sense warned me,' replies Leo. 'Are you working here this morning or is this a social visit?'

'I've just brought some veggies down for the shop,' he answers, 'and I've got to check the pot plants for sale outside but I've got time for a coffee.'

'No, you haven't,' says Giles quickly, before Leo can answer. 'Get back to work. Go on.'

Henry rolls his eyes, makes a comical face, and vanishes. Giles shakes his head.

'I thought it would be easier as they grew up,' he says with naïve wistfulness. 'I just want them to be happy and settled.'

'Well, that's an excellent example of a triumph of hope over experience,' observes Leo. 'But don't give up on it. So shall I contact my mole at Sharpham?'

'Yes,' says Giles. 'Yes. Just to sound them out, and I'll talk to Tessa. I should think she'll be delighted. We're in despair about him at the moment. The trouble is that everyone loves him, he's got loads of friends, but no focus.'

'He's twenty-one,' murmurs Leo.

'I know, but I don't want him to be a grasshopper.'

Leo raises his eyebrows. 'Grasshopper?'

'You know, that apocryphal tale about the grasshopper who spends all summer dancing and having fun while everyone else is working hard preparing for the winter ahead and being sensible.'

For some unaccountable reason, Leo thinks of Alice. 'I think I prefer the ways of the grasshopper,' he says. 'After all, there might be no winter ahead.'

Giles is looking at him curiously and Leo laughs and shakes his head.

'Sorry. Look, I'll make the call and you could check out what kind of courses they do at Cirencester these

170

days. It's a long time since I was there.'

'I'll do that,' says Giles, 'and now I ought to get the shopping home. I'll pay for the coffees on the way out.'

Leo knows that this is Giles's way of thanking him for the interest he's showing in Henry's future and nods his own thanks but makes no attempt to follow him out. Since Alice left he has lost the knack of being content, of facing the days alone. Those few weeks have completely upset the pleasant pattern of his life and he doesn't know how to rediscover that old contentment. How quickly and easily they had fallen back into the familiar ways of companionship. She wanted to revisit all the haunts of their past with the same eagerness and delight she had shown as a child and a girl. He delighted in granting her wishes, revelling in her pleasure and, in the long June evenings, they would sit in the garden under the hawthorn tree, sharing a bottle of wine, and talking. How easy it was to be with her: no expectation, no jealousies, no sibling rivalry, no stress. It was wonderful and irreplaceable. But he couldn't persuade her to stay, she was determined, and remembering that this was how she had always been — here today, gone tomorrow — he accepted it and let her go. And, anyway, the summer holidays had just begun and his family would be coming to stay as usual.

They exchanged a few texts, then there was a longer silence. He assumed she was visiting her own family, and then the letter from Adam came. It was a formal notification sent care of his solicitor's address in Oxford, explaining that his mother, Alice Conway, had died peacefully after a long battle with cancer, surrounded by her family. There was to be no funeral and her ashes would be scattered with her partner's in a private local ceremony. Leo could barely take it in. He felt as if he'd been punched in the gut and he was still standing in the kitchen, holding the letter, when Henry came in. Henry was concerned and Leo simply held the letter out to him. Henry read it. He swore a few times and then came across the kitchen and put his arms round him. Leo stood quite still in the comforting embrace. Henry had spent more time with Alice than anyone else. He'd come down from working in the meadow on the pavilion, pour himself a glass of water, join in whatever was going on in an easy natural way. There was an instant affinity between them and Alice welcomed his company. Her death was a shock to him and, as he hugged Leo, he wept for a few moments, unhampered by conventions. Somehow the boy's grief allowed Leo to share it; they talked about her, mourned her together.

'She didn't want to tell you in case it spoiled everything,' Henry said, trying to comfort him. 'I can understand that, can't you? She wanted it to be like it was when you were all young. It would have changed everything.'

Leo could see that: there would have been a constraint that would have made simple happiness and enjoyment impossible. He hopes that he was able to give Alice all that she hoped for, but this time she's vanished for ever and everything has changed.

Now, as he sits alone, Leo remembers that he hasn't done the crossword, which will give him the excuse to stay a little longer. He orders another Americano and pulls the newspaper towards him.

★ ★ ★

Tessa hears Giles come in and instinctively stiffens, as if she must guard herself against him. How easy it is to destroy innocence and trust. He dumps the shopping bag on the kitchen table and bends to greet Bodger.

'Sorry I took a while,' he says. 'I saw Leo having coffee so I joined him.'

'That's good,' she says, beginning to unpack the bag. 'He needs company at the moment. He's still in shock after Alice.'

She lives in terror that Leo might unintentionally let slip some of the things that she has told him, and she wishes she'd never been so weak as to confide in him about Sebastian. But it's such a relief to talk to someone who doesn't judge. She actually believed, after that morning in the café and then seeing Will and Bea in the Castle, that it would be over: that she'd find it easy to stop the foolish flirtation she'd been enjoying.

But it wasn't so simple. Sebastian wasn't just going to walk away. And to her own shame, she couldn't forget him, push him away. It was flattering to be pursued after all these years; to be desired. It was easier once he'd gone back to London and Giles came home, yet she can't quite give it up. She still waits for his texts, needs that little injection of excitement. It's like a drug. Every time she looks at Giles she feels guilty and ashamed, yet that weird little worm of resentment — that he made her leave the cove, that he works away so much — feeds the sense that she's entitled to a little recompense.

He's talking about Leo, how he's suggested that he might speak to a contact at the Sharpham Estate about Henry, and Tessa looks at him as he puts the packets into the fridge, into the cupboards, and longs suddenly to tell him everything. And the thing is, knowing Giles, he'd probably understand. He's a kind, reasonable man who adores his family and is passionate about his work. From the very beginning he's lived between his job in London, for a magazine, and here, with South West Water: photographing riverbanks, estuaries, beaches, often in helicopters, assessing the rise in the water tables. And all the while they were at the cove, she was able to deal with all that, happy with their children in their little piece of paradise. Then everything changed: the children were no longer small, playing in the rock pools, climbing rocks, paddling, and she was required to leave paradise and find a new life outside in the cold.

Tessa knows she's being pathetic, being a drama queen, but she can't seem to help herself.

'Sometimes,' Leo said once, when she'd dropped in to see him, 'when we have a crisis in our lives it's like a catalyst, uncovering things we thought we'd dealt with long ago. Maybe the move from the cove has reminded you of all you lost when you were a child, and now your revenant is here you've gladly welcomed him to distract you from your grief . . . ' He paused. 'Sorry,' he said. 'I sound like some amateur practising mindfulness. Sorry, Tessa.'

She laughed, recognizing the truth in what he had said, still not knowing how to deal with it. And now she sees that Giles has finished unpacking the shopping. She pulls herself together and tries to concentrate on what he's been telling her.

'That's really kind of Leo,' she says. 'Is it worth checking out the agricultural college? I just wish we could find something to turn him on. I remember that

174

I was like that and then by chance I started house-and dog-sitting, which worked perfectly for me. But it's hardly a great vocation, is it?'

Giles shrugs. 'I'm afraid very few are granted a great vocation but it's important to like what you do, and at least Henry likes to see things grow. Let's start with that.'

Tessa feels a great affection for him, and a corresponding wave of guilt.

'Coffee?' she suggests, needing to offer him something to make up for her betrayal. 'I know you've had one with Leo but I haven't had mine yet.'

'Great,' he says rather absently, sitting at the table, pulling his tablet towards him. 'And I'll just have a look at the website.'

Sebastian is mentioning that he might make another visit to Dartmouth, just a couple of days, but Tessa knows that it's a very different scenario now with Henry and Giles at home. It would be crazy to take such a risk, especially after the meeting with Bea and Will. Sebastian has suggested meeting further afield — Exeter, perhaps — and she can't quite bring herself to say no: to tell him that their foolish flirtation is over. Even in moments of complete fantasy, she's never imagined herself leaving Giles, breaking up her family, so she dithers.

Putting the mugs on the table, she pulls up a chair and sits beside Giles so as to look at the website and concentrate on Henry's future.

18

Summer is over. As Henry walks home he's aware of the subtle change of the season. The air is warm and still, swallows are flocking in the sky, on wires, and hedgerows are hung about with feathery old man's beard. Blackberries have been gathered in for jam-making, the last beans have been picked, and he reflects on how different summer's gentle descent into autumn is compared to spring's turbulent entry into summer. He feels so connected with the world around him, so much a part of it. He wishes he could write about it, put how he feels into words, but he's rubbish at it. At least he can make things grow.

He and Leo have a new plan. Leo wants to make a potager and Henry has been gathering information and making notes as to how it must best be achieved. He senses that this project is to distract Leo from the death of his cousin and he wants to encourage him, to focus his mind away from his grief.

In a way this slightly amuses Henry, since he is aware that Leo is trying to do exactly the same thing: trying to focus Henry's mind on some kind of occupation, a career that will excite him. He knows that they're anxious about him, and that Dad and Leo are hatching up some kind of plot, but he's OK with that. They worry about him because he can't quite conform, which is a bit of a problem now that he's left uni and hasn't found a niche into which he can move. He gets it that they probably don't want him living at home for the unforeseeable future, though he's always had holiday jobs and made a contribution, and of course he'd love to be independent, but he can't quite see how it's to be achieved.

Dad's OK really because he's never had a nine-to-five job and he's prepared to admit that there are all kinds of ways of making a living. And Ma, well, she's all over the place at the minute and secretly he's a bit worried about her. He talked to Charlotte about it when she was home during the holidays — when she wasn't off with her boyfriend and his family — but she's too distracted by her own life to really get it.

'It's probably the menopause,' she said dismissively. 'She's fine.'

Which is all very well but he can't quite believe it. He knows Ma didn't want to move from the cove, and he understands, but she's changed from being a bit moody and depressed to a kind of instability: jokey one minute and then kind of preoccupied, and then doing the motherly thing as if she's been neglecting them. Ever since Alice died so unexpectedly, he's had a new fear: that Ma is ill, that she's got something wrong with her and she's not telling him. But he's noticed that she's the same with Dad, who just goes on being his normal self, and surely he wouldn't behave like that if Ma were seriously ill. All the same, the fear persists and he's glad that Dad's going to be around for a bit, which might make things right again.

Henry knows how lucky he is to have good friends with whom he was at school in Kingsbridge, but most of them are at uni or starting new jobs, and he misses Clara a bit but not enough to wish they were still together. But on these golden evenings he finds it hard simply to go indoors and leave the magic of it all. It seems such a waste, so he will go home, collect

Bodger and walk down to the beach.

Something Alice had said, as they stood together in the wildflower meadow, comes into his mind. 'They are not long, the days of wine and roses.' He looked down at her — she wasn't very tall — and her face was sad, but that other look was there, too. He can't quite describe it to himself but there was a kind of luminous glow in her brown eyes that spoke of joy and hope. Even to himself this sounds silly, but he can't think how else to express it. It made him feel good; just being with her was life-affirming.

Now, of course, the words have a deeper meaning and he knows he must not waste a single minute of his life. It is her legacy to him. He's so glad now he and Leo built the little pavilion in her favourite place in the meadow, placing it where it looks across the land to the sea beyond. How she encouraged them, sharing in the design, in the pretty blue-grey colour of the paint, the choosing of a small table to place beside the bench that runs along the back wall. Small folding chairs could be brought up in the summer, the perfect place for a drink. Henry is so glad that it was such a success. It will be his memorial to her.

★　★　★

'Where's he off to this time?' asks Bea, as she sees Henry crossing the courtyard and going off with Bodger. 'He's never still, that boy.'

'Can't blame him on an evening like this. You should be glad he doesn't just want to sit around indoors staring at a screen or on his phone,' answers Will. 'Apparently that's what the young do these days. Young Henry has got all the makings.'

'Of what?' asks Bea sharply.

She finds it difficult that Henry isn't using his degree to find himself a good job, instead continuing to work part time at Stokeley and help Leo in his projects.

'Give him time,' says Will. 'He just hasn't found his place yet.'

Bea rolls her eyes. Experience has taught her that boys will be idle unless they're pushed, and she's not sure that either Giles or Tessa is doing enough. Giles is such a gentle soul and Tessa . . . Well, Tessa is still in a very odd mood: mooning around, preoccupied.

'Do you think Tessa is still seeing that man?' she asks abruptly.

They've been over this several times since the meeting in the Royal Castle. Will sighs. They were so certain that meeting had restored Tessa to her senses that it's rather worrying to watch her in this odd, distracted state.

'How would I know?' Anxiety makes him irritable. 'But I can't see how. The kids have been home for the holidays and Giles has been back for most of that time. How could she have the opportunity?'

'Perhaps that's why she's behaving so strangely,' says Bea. 'Perhaps she's missing him.'

She sounds sad and Will hastens to comfort her.

'She loves Giles. I know she does. She's just having a silly five minutes. After all, she was engaged to Sebastian when she met Giles, wasn't she? And Giles won.'

'But that's probably the trouble. This old friend and lover turns up, she hasn't seen him for years, and she can have a bit of fun with him. Meet up for coffee, talk about old times, and then suddenly she remembers all the things she liked about him the first

179

time around. She's at a susceptible age and here's this good-looking man paying her attention.'

'But she chose Giles,' argues Will. 'And I can't believe that she's regretting it. Not really. Sebastian's just turned her head a bit. And from that point of view I think it's very good that Henry's around at the moment, as well as Giles. Between us we can get her through it.'

Bea nods reluctantly: she's not convinced. She hears a clattering behind her and turns away from the window. Will is busy at the table.

'Scrabble,' he says. 'It's a long time since you beat me at Scrabble. Chance to get your own back.' He grins at her and holds out the bag of tiles. 'You can go first.'

19

The card arrives a few days later. Leo hears the letterbox clang and he gets up from his breakfast and walks through the study and into the hall. There are a few circulars and a square handwritten envelope lying on the mat. He picks them all up and carries them back to the kitchen. He puts the circulars in the recycling pile and, sitting down again, he studies the envelope. Dizzy Gillespie is playing 'They Can't Take That Away From Me'. Leo doesn't recognize the handwriting but there's an Oxford postmark and his heart beats a little faster as he seizes a knife and slits open the envelope.

The card is beautiful. A watercolour of wildflowers, blue, scarlet, gold, cream, and he opens it hurriedly, glancing at the address and then at the signature. The address is merely The Old Dairy but the signature is a flourish: Maya. Quickly he begins to read her message.

Dear Leo,
Do you mind if I call you Leo? It's what Granny always called you. Only I promised I would write to you for her. She hoped you would allow a little part of her to come back to you, so when we scattered her ashes with Grandpa's I kept some aside in a little box that she loved. Are you OK with this? If you are, perhaps I could bring them down? She told me so much about her holidays with you, and she was so happy when she came back this last time, as if

181

something really special had happened. If it's all right with you I'd really like to see where Granny was so happy. I can come on the train and stay in a B & B. My phone number is at the top. Please say yes.
    Maya x

Leo rereads her letter. Then, holding it, he crosses his arms, rests his forehead on them and weeps. Not for very long, but the relief is overwhelming. He'd talked with Alice about the guilt he suffered after the wedding, how he tried to track her down, and she was shocked that he'd taken so much to himself.

'But it wasn't your fault, old Lion,' she cried. 'You didn't get me pregnant. I wasn't your responsibility. What could you have done? Good grief! You were the same age as Henry is now — younger. Not yet twenty-one and still at college. I shouldn't have just run away. But it was what I always did when things got tough. And what could be done about it anyway? George was happily married to my cousin — not that I would have wanted to marry George. There was nothing between us, except friendship and that one crazy moment of foolish comfort. But why you should bear any part of the blame I can't imagine.'

She talked on, telling him about Jason, and how she loved him, how happy they were, and at last some of Leo's pain dissolved, though he still regretted his inaction on that day long ago, that he allowed her to go, alone and afraid. He raises his head and rereads the card. This he can do: a part of Alice will return to Long Orchard, this time for ever, and Maya will come with her.

He seizes his phone and dials the number at the top of the card. He listens to it ring, his heart beating

182

fast, but there is no answer and he is bitterly, foolishly, disappointed. But there is a voicemail and he takes a deep breath and talks.

'This is Leo, Maya. I've had your card. Thank you. It's so good to hear from you. Yes, please, I'd love to meet you and you'd be very welcome to stay here at Long Orchard if you'd like to. I can pick you up from the train at Totnes if you let me know when. Goodbye.'

He sits for a moment, not knowing what to do next. He reads the card again, and then looks at the wildflowers: blue cornflowers, scarlet and yellow poppies, delicate lady's smock, pink campion, and he wonders if Alice chose the card, ready for just this moment: that she planned this so that he should not feel that she had forgotten him.

It was so hard to be excluded from those last rites, though he could never have imagined a solemn church funeral for her, and he could imagine that Alice herself would not have wanted George and Helen there.

'Adam must never meet George,' she had said.

Remembering, he feels a tiny clutch of fear at his heart. Supposing Helen and George should decide to visit while Maya is here? How much does she know? He can imagine why Alice didn't want George to meet his son, but what about his granddaughter? Leo tries to think it through. Clearly, Alice planned this meeting knowing the dangers, and he must simply go with the flow. Nothing shall stop Maya travelling to Long Orchard with her precious cargo and he must wait for her, just as he waited for Alice. A text pops in and he stares at it with disbelief and dismay.

Hi Leo. Down just for a few days. Couldn't resist another little visit. Any chance we could meet for coffee? Em x

Leo groans aloud. This is the last thing he needs. But this time there's no question of politeness and prevarication. He taps out a reply:

So sorry. People staying, very busy for the foreseeable future. Enjoy your stay. Leo

He feels rattled and he cannot simply sit still. He'll go for a walk on the beach and make a plan. He wonders how soon Maya will come, which room she should have. Leo puts on his boots, takes his jacket from the peg and hurries away to the sea.

★ ★ ★

Tessa is sitting in the café at Bayards Cove. She simply cannot help herself. It is as if, ever since she met Sebastian by chance, she's been possessed by something that won't let her rest, that whispers in her ear, makes her discontented.

It's like I'm mad, she thinks. I probably am. But what can I do?

She looks around her. Now that summer is over, the grockles are gone and the café is not quite so busy. The young mums with their babies are here on the sofas, the elderly man is bent over his crossword, but there is no Em with her laptop in the alcove.

Leo told her that Em had gone back to London. He was embarrassed by the way things turned out, that he hadn't seen it coming, but he still believed that it wasn't too serious on Em's part.

'I think she just got carried away by being in Dartmouth, out of her normal routines, and it was like one

184

of those silly holiday romances you always regret.'

Tessa grinned at him. 'Sounds like you speak from experience?' she suggested, and he laughed.

'I wish,' he said. 'There was a bit of a showdown between Bethany and Jenny when they came down. I overheard it: Jenny telling Bethany off for encouraging Em. It was only then that I realized they actually thought I was encouraging her, too, and had come down to check me out. It was all totally surreal. Poor Bethany went away with her tail between her legs, and not long after that, Em went back to London. I think she was going, anyway. It was only a short sabbatical but I never found out if she finished her play. I feel cross with myself for being so dense but I decided not to get in touch with her in case it gave the wrong idea.'

Tessa can't help smiling as she remembers Leo's expression, and how they'd laughed together, though he was still feeling rather guilty.

Which is typical of Leo, thinks Tessa. It's his default mode.

Each time the café door opens she glances towards it, a tiny flicker of hope in her heart. But Sebastian doesn't come and it's crazy to expect him to. If he were to be down here, he'd text her. They still text: silly little non-committal messages, except that he always adds 'Missing you, kiddo' at the end.

Her thoughts drift back to Leo, and to Alice. She met them by chance, in the lane just after she asked Henry to invite them to supper. Alice and Leo were walking back from the beach, talking together, deep in conversation, and as she approached with Bodger she saw them stop and turn to each other, bursting into laughter. They looked so happy that she was smiling as she walked towards them. They greeted her, Leo

185

introduced her, and Alice beamed.

'So you are Henry's mother,' she said. 'I have to tell you that I am totally in love with Henry.'

Tessa shook her head. 'Join the queue,' she said. 'Everyone is in love with him. It's hopeless and very bad for him. He's a spoilt brat, really.'

'Come in and have coffee,' Leo suggested. 'We were going to stop off at Seabreeze but the café is really busy. How about it?'

'I'd love to,' she answered, curious to meet this woman about whom Henry was so enthusiastic. 'If that's OK.'

They hurried her in with them and she watched with interest to see Leo so happy, jolted out of his usual calm, self-contained ways by this vivacious woman. She must be about the same age as he was, Tessa guessed, but she was so charming that she seemed ageless. In her long cotton skirt and her loose shirt, a straw hat on her head, she had a youthful, bohemian quality. Leo sat them at the table under the hawthorn tree and went to make the coffee.

'Leo told me about you,' Tessa said. 'That you're cousins and you used to stay here as a child.'

Alice nodded, stroking Bodger, who was sitting beside her, his head on her knee.

'It seems unchanged,' she said. 'Except for the wild-flower meadow and the arboretum. That's all new, of course. Has Henry told you of our plan to build a little summer house up in the meadow? Nothing grand, of course, more like a shed, but somewhere to sit and enjoy the meadow and the view. Henry is going to help. What a lovely boy he is. You must be very proud of him.'

Tessa felt a mix of gratitude, pride and embarrassment. 'He's causing us anxiety at the moment,' she admitted. 'He can't seem to find his niche and we don't know how to encourage him.'

Alice gave a little sigh, and her gaze drifted as if she were remembering times past.

'I don't think I ever had a niche,' she said wistfully. 'I never seemed quite to belong. It was as if I'd been dropped into a world where I didn't know the language or the rules. I tried so many things until I realized that I was simply running away from myself. Jason grounded me. He tethered me to this strange universe in which I found myself and helped me to make sense of it. Of a small part of it, anyway.'

Tessa was silent, watching her, unusually moved.

'He must have been rather special,' she said at last.

'Oh, he was,' Alice said, smiling. 'He was a nurturer. He loved to see things grow, to create beautiful spaces. My dear old aunt Hattie — she was my mother's oldest sister — left me her little cottage when she died. Jason could hardly believe how lucky he was. It had a garden that was very overgrown and he brought it back to life.'

Tessa saw that her eyes were brimming with tears and instinctively she reached across and covered the thin hands locked together on the table with her own. They looked at each other, totally connected in this moment. No words were needed; they would have been superfluous.

'Your Henry reminds me of Jason,' Alice said at last, wiping her cheeks with her fingers. 'He has the same qualities. Everything will become clear.'

Tessa nodded. At that moment in the garden, she felt a sense of peace. All would be well. Leo came out carrying the tray, they talked about the proposed supper party and the moment passed, but the peace remained.

Now, sitting in the café, Tessa tries to regain that sense of peace she'd felt in Alice's company. The shock of her death was great. Leo was silent with grief, but Henry, too, was shocked and rather quiet in his first experience of the reality of it: the finality of death. He was determined to create something to honour Alice. There was the little pavilion, of course, the wooden, blue-grey-painted, open-fronted structure with its seat looking out on to the wildflower meadow. That would always be special, but more was needed, and now he and Leo are planning a potager, which Alice also talked about. There was something special, she said, about seeing flowers and vegetables growing together: sweet peas climbing with the runner beans, nasturtiums amongst the carrots and lettuces. Needing something to focus his own mind away from his grief, and to console Henry, Leo suggested it, and Henry responded with enthusiasm.

Thank God for Leo, thinks Tessa. Another nurturer. She wonders, as she has so many times, why he and Jenny separated. Having seen him with his cousin, so happy, so much on top form, she feels another stab of sorrow that this has been taken from him.

'It's odd,' she once said to Giles, 'that Leo hasn't found another woman. He's such a lovely guy.'

'I think that Leo is one of those people who doesn't necessarily need to be in a relationship,' Giles answered. 'He's not emotional, he's not needy, and he has a very close-knit family. He's always got a project going on, he loves his jazz — I think that Leo is a very contented man.'

Contentment, thinks Tessa. The greatest gift of

all. Not joy, not passion, not lust — all so ephemeral — but contentment.

Rather like that sense of peace she shared with Alice in the garden at Long Orchard. But how to find it and, having found it, keep hold of it? Stop hankering after Sebastian: that would be a start.

Tessa puts her phone in her bag and even as she does so, a message comes in. It's from Sebastian:

Hi kiddo. Might you be around if I'm down your way next week? X

She stares at it. She wants to type 'Yes', knows she should say 'No'. But she can't bring herself to make that final gesture. On impulse she replies:

Tuesday. Same place. Same time.

She pushes her phone into her bag, gets up and goes out into the town.

20

Driving to the station, Leo is tense with nervousness. After all the excitement, the plans, hearing Maya's voice, he is suddenly aware of what a big thing this is. He is going to meet Alice's granddaughter, who is grieving yet full of expectation. Leo wonders how he will cope with the emotional time ahead; how he will connect with a girl he's never met and what common ground they will have. Clearly Alice is the connection but he can see all the problems now where there was just the simple joy of meeting this girl who looks like the Alice of his youth and who sounds so sweet and lively.

He's spent some time wondering whether he should enjoin Henry in this important first meeting but eventually decided against it. It might be nice for Maya to have another young person around but, then again, it's a complication explaining who Henry is and why he's there when Maya might be nervous and emotional. It's so impossible to get it right. And nobody knows the undercurrents; the fact that Maya is George's granddaughter. He hears again Alice's injunction: 'Adam must never meet George,' yet she decided to risk Maya meeting George. Having been shown the photos on Alice's phone he can see that Adam's likeness to George is unmistakable, whilst Maya, quite apart from being female, has no clear resemblance to him. Yet there are risks and Leo's head is full of them as he drives down the hill and into the station car park.

He parks the car and walks out on to the platform. The overhead announcements show that the train is on time and will be arriving in twelve minutes. He's texted her that he's on his way and will be waiting for her and she's replied with an emoji indicating happiness. He has a feeling that she and Henry will get along very well and he's glad that there's a young person around. Henry can't wait to meet her and is on standby in case Leo needs reinforcements.

'It will depend on what kind of state she's in,' he explained to Henry. 'She seems very happy to be coming down, but obviously it's a very emotional occasion so I don't want to pre-empt anything. But I want you to meet her, of course.'

He's also explained the situation to Tessa and Giles, who are also standing by in case they can be of any use.

'Poor child,' Tessa said. 'I think it's very brave of her to come alone to strangers to do this for her granny. Let us know if there's anything at all we can do.'

Leo decided that Maya should have Alice's room, and he made it clean and fresh, finding a frame for an old photo of Alice sitting on an upturned hull of a wooden dinghy down on the beach, laughing at the camera. She was about seventeen, long hair over her shoulders, bare legs braced to keep her balance. Beside it on the small chest, Leo placed a small silver vase with the last of the sweet peas. He stood staring around the room, wondering if she'd like it and if there's anything he'd forgotten, and he's still mentally checking when the train slides in and there's the usual commotion of announcements, hurrying people, and doors opening.

Leo looks along the platform towards the back

of the train, then back to the front, and here she is, almost running towards him, with such a familiar air of vitality and expectation that it's as if he's meeting Alice way back, arriving for the holidays, full of excitement and hopefulness. Instinctively he goes towards her, holding out his arms, and then feels foolish. But she is here, putting down her bags and clutching him, hugging him, as if she has known him for ever.

'Leo,' she cries, looking up at him, eyes brimming. 'I knew you at once. Isn't that amazing? And you knew me, didn't you?'

'Yes,' he says, smiling at her, releasing her, picking up the bags. 'But I have seen a photo, you know. And I bet you have, too. It's not quite magic.'

She laughs, walking beside him to the car. 'That's very prosaic of you. I prefer to think of it as magic.'

'You do that,' he says, opening the door for her, trying not to stare at her lest he should embarrass her.

'Granny did show me a photo she took when she was here. She was so happy, Leo. It hurts that she's not here any more.'

He closes the door, goes round to the driver's side, and gets in.

'It's terrible,' he says, putting the keys into the ignition. 'It's cruel and terrible but we have to get on with it somehow. And this — you coming here, and giving me the chance to show you where she was so happy — is a step towards that.' He hesitates, his hand still on the keys, staring forward at where the train is still standing. 'Or am I being prosaic again?'

At once she laughs. 'Yes, you are, but Granny warned me about you, so it's OK. I know that it's no good weeping and wailing all over you and expecting sympathy.'

Leo lets out a huge, silent breath of relief. He's taken a chance and it's come off.

'That's OK, then,' he says. 'So now I know that you're prepared for the worst, let's go home.'

He drives out of the station yard, up the hill and away towards Dartmouth. He's pleased that Maya is an easy companion. She is taking in her surroundings, alert to the places that have been described to her by Alice, and she is relaxed. He quickly realizes that although she is much like her grandmother, the vulnerability is missing. Despite that first emotional meeting, Maya is in no way out of her depth. Leo remembers Alice telling him that when she was fifteen and her parents relocated from London to New York, Maya became a boarder at her school in Berkshire. She was used to coping, to travelling to and fro and fending for herself. They are all very proud that she's done well in her exams and has gained a place at Cambridge.

'You must meet Henry,' Leo says, following this train of thought. 'He's just finished uni and he's deciding what to do next.'

Maya is staring out of the window but she turns to smile at him. 'Yes, I'd like to,' she says. 'Granny told me about Henry.'

Nothing more than that, no special enthusiasm or polite comments, and Leo's respect for her deepens. Maya will make up her own mind about Henry. Now, she's exclaiming in wonder at her first sight of the sea, of steep cliffs and small coves, and Start Bay in the distance.

'Wow,' she breathes. 'That is insane.' And he has to remember that in the vocabulary of the young the word denotes all that is amazing.

She opens the window, breathing in great gulps of salty air, her hair blowing around her face, and once again she is like Alice: childlike, enthusiastic, filled with joyful wonder at unexpected beauty. He remembers that she used to say: 'We are as big or small as the objects of our love' and he is filled with gratitude for this third chance, and with trepidation lest he should fail again.

'It's pretty special, isn't it?' And he sees her smile at his ineptitude. He's glad that the sun is shining, that the scenery is doing its best for him. He has a proprietorial feeling for this stretch of the coast and he's pleased that it's really putting on a show. He points out the places Alice might have mentioned — Blackpool Sands, Start Bay lighthouse, Slapton Ley — telling little stories of the past, and then they are driving through the village, up the hill and through the open gateway. Maya sits looking around her, at the house, into the garden, and Leo gets out and goes round to open her door. She smiles up at him as she gets out, and he smiles back at her, suddenly full of confidence.

'Welcome home, Maya,' he says.

* * *

She follows him into the house, looking about her, remembering how Granny described it to her.

'It was home to me,' Alice had said. 'I was a bit like you, away at school, father abroad, and it was my still centre.'

Maya can get that. It must have been much worse for Granny, with her mother dying so young, how she was passed around in the holidays, and she's glad that they made this plan together, that Maya should bring some part of her back to where she was so happy. Seeing Leo waiting for her at the station has touched Maya's heart. She knows she looks like Granny and can guess how hard it is for him to have her here after the shock of the awful news.

'I couldn't tell him,' Granny said. 'I chickened out, Maya. We were being so happy and I hated the thought of spoiling it. I was a coward. And now I'm putting it all on to you and expecting you to be strong where I was weak.'

But now she knows all of the truth, Maya realizes that Granny was strong, too, way back then: young, alone, expecting a child. It was a shock to know that her father was not Grandpa Jason's son. Holding Maya's hand tightly, Granny told her the truth, of the man called George, who was her friend, of how in a moment of loneliness and weakness they'd comforted each other, which was how Maya's father was conceived.

'George never knew,' she said. 'He still doesn't, and they must never meet. Adam would guess at once. It would be like looking in a mirror. But a part of me is sad that George doesn't know he has a granddaughter. Sad that he doesn't know you. There might come a time when you might need each other and I decided that you should know the truth. I don't know if there might be a way . . .'

She was too exhausted to talk any more and lay back on her pillows, Maya's hand still grasped in her own.

Now, Maya follows Leo through the house and up the stairs. He opens a door and anxiously watches her reaction. She looks around her with pleasure.

'This is Granny's room,' she says. 'Isn't it? She

described it to me, and how you can see the sea across the fields.'

She smells the sweet peas, picks up the photograph and studies it. How young Granny looks, how happy. Maya puts the photo back and turns to smile at Leo, touched by his thoughtfulness and by his love for his cousin.

'I love it,' she says. 'Thank you.' But she hesitates and his expression changes.

'What?' he asks.

She shakes her head, cross with herself. 'Nothing,' she says.

'What?' he asks again, more insistently.

'It's silly,' she says. 'You mustn't laugh. Or be cross. It's just sometimes, when Granny was talking about you she'd call you 'old Lion'. It was always very affectionate and, just for a minute there, I almost said it myself. I nearly said, 'Thank you, old Lion.' Sorry.'

But to her amazement and horror, his eyes fill with tears.

'I wish you had,' he says. 'That would be wonderful if you ever felt you wanted to, or that you could.' He blinks the tears away, smiling, embarrassed. 'Sorry,' he says. 'Sorry, Maya. I'm being a fool. You must be needing something to eat and drink after the journey. Come down when you're ready.'

He goes out, closing the door behind him, and she wants to rush after him and hug him, but knows that it's not the right moment. Pausing at intervals to look around her, she opens her bags and begins to unpack them.

21

Henry waits eagerly for his summons to Long Orchard. He knows that Maya has arrived. Leo has texted to say that she's safely there and looking forward to seeing him. He reflects on this: it's kind of Leo to keep him in the loop. He understands how much it means to Henry after his friendship with Alice, the fun they had in building the little pavilion, and the little opening ceremony when the three of them carried wine and nibbles up on a lovely starry night, Alice lit some candles and they listened to the sea's restless music.

It's odd how it's possible to become so fond of someone so quickly and how terrible then to know that person is gone for ever. He gives a sigh. Bodger, always quick to notice someone in distress, comes to sit beside him and drops his head comfortingly on his knee. Henry fondles the long silky ears and murmurs to him, quelling the desire to take him for a walk along the lane, past Long Orchard, in the hope of catching a glimpse of Leo and his guest.

'That's the third sigh in the last ten minutes,' observes his father. 'What's the problem?'

'Nothing,' answers Henry quickly. 'Just deciding what to do. It was a bit quiet at Stokeley so I'm home early. Want a cup of tea?'

It's odd having Dad back again, at home between shoots, suddenly appearing unexpectedly.

'Yes, thanks,' his father answers. 'Your mum's round next door so I expect she'll be having one with them. Haven't you got some project on with Leo?'

'Yes, but he's got Maya arriving today so I thought I'd give them time to settle in,' says Henry, filling the kettle, putting it on the Rayburn.

'That's sensible,' says Dad, sitting at the table and taking Henry's place with Bodger.

Henry turns round, leaning back against the rail, looking at his father, and suddenly he decides to speak out.

'Have you noticed that Ma's being a bit weird lately, Dad?' he says tentatively. 'She seems all over the place. Is something wrong?'

'Wrong?' His father frowns. 'How d'you mean, wrong? Do you mean between us? There's nothing as far as I know. She's still feeling it, having to move from the cove — '

'Yes, I know that,' Henry breaks in impatiently, 'but it's not that. This is different. I'm just wondering . . . She's not ill or anything, is she, and you're not telling me because you don't want to worry me?'

He feels huge relief at voicing this fear he's had ever since he heard about Alice. Alice hadn't said anything but he knows now that she knew she was going to die. There were so many clues if only he'd had the wit to see them. But his father is looking at him in surprise and a kind of horror.

'Of course not,' he says. 'I promise you we would tell you anything like that. Good God, of course we would. You're not a child. What a horrible thing for you to have been thinking. Your mother is perfectly fine. But I agree that she seems a bit off colour. Actually, I've been wondering if we should go away for a bit. Have a complete change of scene.'

Henry's relief is so great he feels quite weak. He's allowed this secret dread to get to him and as he makes the tea his hands are quite shaky.

'Sounds like a really good idea,' he says. 'I can look after Bodger and keep an eye on Wilby.'

His father smiles at the familiar nickname.

'I'm really sorry you've had this on your mind,' he says. 'I'll talk to your mum and we'll make a plan.'

'Great,' Henry says, happy with relief. 'Cake?'

★ ★ ★

Giles is still sitting at the table when Tessa comes back from next door and he looks up at her as she bends to stroke Bodger, and glances at the plates.

'Celebrating?' she asks.

He grins and nods. 'You could say that. I've had one of my great ideas and Henry and I were celebrating.'

'Really?' She raises her eyebrows. 'Am I allowed to know what it is?'

'Definitely,' he says. 'It can't happen without you. Do you want some tea?'

'I've had some,' she answers, sitting down opposite. 'So what's the great thought for the day?'

'Henry and I were thinking that you seem the least bit stressed. Not quite your usual cheerful self, and we decided that what you need is a holiday. A complete change of scene. He says he'll look after things here. What d'you think?'

He watches her, slightly puzzled by her reaction. She looks almost alarmed, wary, and Giles begins to feel anxious. He thinks about what Henry said and decides to be honest.

'Actually, Henry's worried that you might be ill but not telling us, and I said that you would never do that.'

199

He hesitates. 'You wouldn't, would you?'

It's clear that she can see the fear in his face and she answers quickly.

'No, of course I wouldn't. I'm fine, I promise you. What a terrible idea.'

'Yes, it is, but it shows how worried he is, and so am I. I know it's been a tough time for you, darling, but I hoped you might be adjusting a bit. In fact, it seems the opposite. Can you tell me what's wrong?'

Her look is compounded of alarm, misery, and a kind of gratefulness for his concern.

'I don't know,' she falters. 'It's just . . . I'm just in a difficult place, Giles. I'm OK really, honestly. It's just been a bad year for me — well, you know all that stuff — but I can't seem to get over it.'

She looks away from him, as if she's concealing something, unable to meet his eyes, and he has a sudden terrible suspicion that she might be having an affair. The idea is shocking but he's been away so much, and she's been unhappy since they left the cove.

'Is there someone else?' He blurts it out, unable to wrap it up, and once again sees that indefinable look flash across her face. 'Are you having an affair?'

'No,' she says quickly: almost too quickly. Then more gently, 'No, I'm not having an affair, Giles, I promise you.'

'But there's something, isn't there? You can tell me, darling. Whatever it is. Or should I say, whoever it is.'

He is completely thrown off balance by the conversation but he reaches his hand across the table to her and, after a moment, she takes it.

'It's Sebastian,' she says. She gives a deep sigh, slumps a little, as if she's setting down a heavy load. 'Sebastian was down visiting his son at the naval college, and we bumped into each other. We had coffee and did the old times thing. It was good to see him, so we met again a couple of times.' He lets go of her hand and she shakes her head. 'It's silly, and it's not going anywhere, but it just felt good to have someone taking notice of me. Oh God. What do I sound like?'

He watches her, shocked. He remembers Sebastian very well. Tessa always insisted that she and Sebastian both had doubts about whether they should get married, that they were both grateful for the odd twist of fate that brought Giles into their lives and gave them an escape route out of their engagement. Giles has never had a reason to doubt this, but now, suddenly, he's assailed with a terrible idea. Perhaps Tessa has loved Sebastian all along and now, meeting him again, has realized her mistake.

'Met a few times?' he asks sharply. 'Met where?'

She puts her elbows on the table, rubs her fingers around her eyes. 'I told you. For coffee. In Bayards Cove.'

'And that's all?'

This time she looks at him, a puzzled but almost guilty look, and he is angry; angry and jealous and utterly confused by the strength of these emotions.

'Of course it's all,' she says. 'I told you. Look, it was just good to see him again. I've known him for ever, and his family were so kind to me. And I know it was probably wrong but it was nice to meet with someone of my own generation and be able to laugh and be a bit silly. That's all.'

'And when was the last time?' he demands.

She stares at him, clearly surprised by an anger she's never seen before.

'Not for weeks,' she answers. And then suddenly

she is angry, too. 'For Christ's sake! I told you it was just a cup of coffee and a bit of a laugh. Are you telling me that you've never done that with one of the girls on the team when you're away on an assignment? Do you never sit and relax and have a bit of fun with an attractive woman? Seriously? Do you never feel a bit lonely and crave the company of someone your own age rather than two old people, two teenagers and a dog?'

'I might,' he answers. 'Yes, very possibly I do. But not with someone I was in love with and engaged to be married to. It's a bit different, isn't it?'

'But can't you see that that's the whole point? It's not like I met someone new and was attracted to him. It's simply because it *was* Sebastian, an old friend, someone with a shared past that I could talk to easily without constraints. Yes, of course, there was a flirtatious side to it, but it was much more to do with the company.'

She stops, slumps back in her chair as if she is defeated. Something in her expression and body language unexpectedly disarms him. She isn't defensive now, which might have indicated guilt, or that she's indignant that he should suspect her, but it's that she's miserable, and he begins to understand how Sebastian might have knocked her off balance in her vulnerable state, given her the attention and company that he himself has not been providing during this last year. Slowly, his anger simmers down a little. It's not in his nature to sustain it, but he's had a shock and he needs to step back. He doesn't really fear Sebastian. He defeated him once and he can do it again. But he mustn't underestimate him, or patronize her. He can think of nothing that doesn't trivialize what she's said and he's still battling with his own anger and jealousy.

'Thank you for telling me,' he says at last.

Tessa shrugs, makes a little face. 'It was nothing, Giles. Truly. Loneliness, vanity.' She looks at him. 'If you want to know, I feel a complete prat.'

There's a little silence. Giles knows that some kind of gesture must be made but it's difficult to know what. He goes back to his conversation with Henry.

'Do you think perhaps we should give ourselves a break and go away for a few days?' he suggests. He doesn't want it to sound cheesy, a second honeymoon, that would put way too much pressure on it, but at the same time it's a test. Will she want to go away with him? 'We could go to Cornwall, down on the north coast?'

He waits and at last she nods, and takes a deep breath.

'I'd like that,' she says.

He feels relieved and the tension between them relaxes a little. 'How about a drink?' he suggests. 'It's a bit early but as my old ma says, 'The sun's always over the yardarm somewhere."

She nods again and then suddenly she brightens. 'That's what we'll do,' she says. 'We'll go down to Cornwall. We could drop in on Kate on the way. See the family down on the Tamar. And then spend a few days on our own together. That's just what I need at the moment. Do you think we could do that?'

Giles can hardly believe this can be so simple a remedy, but it's a good start. He gets up to collect glasses.

'Of course we can,' he answers. 'I think perhaps it's what we both need.'

He still feels angry, but he knows that he must contain it. He's ashamed that he hasn't noticed how difficult Tessa has been finding all the recent changes in her life or how much she's missed him. He's been wrong in assuming that the company of Will and Bea is enough.

He puts the drink beside her, bends and lightly kisses the top of her head. He knows that this is just the beginning of the way back and that he must take nothing for granted.

* * *

Tessa remains where she is when Giles goes out to take a call from a colleague. She feels exhausted, as if she has passed through some huge ordeal, but relief is beginning to make itself felt. She hadn't realized what a strain it's been, keeping secrets, deceiving the people closest to her, and she knows how lucky she is that Giles is the kind of man he is. She feels guilty that she's behaved so foolishly, grateful for his generous response. The plan to go away is a good one, though she feels slightly anxious about being alone with Giles under these new circumstances, as if it might be some kind of test, but she senses that her readiness to agree to it has gone some way to proving to him that there is nothing serious in this resurrected friendship with Sebastian.

She's still alone, thinking about this when Henry and Bodger come into the kitchen. She can see that Henry's looking cheerful, even excited, but his expression changes a little as he looks at her. She remembers what Giles told her and she is filled with remorse. To think that Henry has been imagining that she might have some incurable disease is terrible and she smiles at him.

'I think it's you I have to thank for a brilliant idea,' she says, stroking Bodger.

Henry's clearly taken aback. 'Is it?' he says. 'I'm not sure brilliant ideas are my thing. What was it?'

She laughs. 'Your father said you thought it was time we both took a holiday and on serious reflection, coupled with several glasses of wine, we've decided that you're right.'

He looks surprised and then pleased. 'Really? That's amazing.'

'It's time,' she says. 'I've been grumping around, feeling sorry for myself, and we both agree that we'll take ourselves off just for a few days before Dad's next assignment.'

'Sounds good to me,' he says, opening the fridge, bringing out one of his energy drinks. 'So where will you go?'

She's finding this easier than she thought, as if being honest with Giles has cleared her vision, and restored some of the old values.

'You'll laugh when I tell you,' she warns him, and he grins at her as he tilts the bottle and takes a swig from it.

'Don't tell me,' he says. 'You're going paragliding in the Andes. Reindeer-watching in Lapland.'

She shakes her head. 'Nowhere near,' she says ruefully. 'Sorry to disappoint you but we're going to Cornwall, down to the north coast. We can drop in and see Kate.'

'Seriously?' He stares at her. 'But that's great, actually. Granny's really cool. You'll have fun with her and all those crazy friends of hers and you can see Uncle Guy and all of them down on the Tamar.'

'Yes,' says Tessa, and suddenly is confident that this

205

is exactly what she needs.

She needs that group of people who are her extended family: especially Kate who gave her so much support when she was young and alone, before she had ever met Giles. Kate has never seemed like a mother-in-law just a wise, loving friend. A reconnection with Kate might just restore her perspective. Tessa guesses that it won't be quite that easy, that she'll miss the crazy rush of adrenalin, the thrill of the secret, the fun of an unexpected text, but it's a beginning. Now it just remains for her to tell Sebastian.

Henry is watching her. 'So you're OK, then?' he says casually, but she is not deceived.

'I'm absolutely fine, I promise,' she says. 'I just need a change of scene. You were spot on about that.'

'Good,' he says, hesitates, then says with a seeming indifference, 'They are not long, the days of wine and roses'.'

Tessa is silent for a moment, trying to place the quote and wondering what has inspired him to say it. She decides to play it cool.

'You'd better believe it,' she says. 'So what were you grinning at when you came in?'

All his anxiety and concern are swept away and his face lights up.

'I've had a text from Leo,' he tells her. 'Maya's arrived and he's invited me over to meet her tomorrow morning.'

He looks so pleased that Tessa is delighted for him and she thinks of something Kate says in moments of excitement.

"O frabjous day! Callooh! Callay!' Let joy be unconfined,' she says.

Henry rolls his eyes. 'How much wine did you say

you've had?'

Tessa laughs. She feels unexpectedly light-hearted. 'Not quite enough,' she says. 'Pass the bottle across and tell me some more about Maya.'

22

Maya sits on her bed, holding the carved wooden box on her knees, running her thumbs over the raised patterns. It was quite easy to scoop the ashes from the bigger container just before they were to be scattered with Grandpa Jason's in the orchard he had created. It was Granny's wish and Maya had no scruple in carrying it out, just as she has come here to Leo without telling her father, who is too involved in the divorce to care much anyway. He knew that Maya was to inherit the little cottage, which pleased him because his daughter would be provided for and it wouldn't become part of the bargaining stakes in the settlement.

As she sits there, Maya is surprised that she isn't more upset about the divorce — yet it was always a volatile relationship; both her parents had affairs. She was quite relieved when the Bank posted her father to New York. She was happy at school: she enjoyed the work, the friendship of both boys and girls, and her visits to the little cottage in Oxford for exeats and half-terms, though New York was the most amazing experience, too. It was just a pity that those visits were accompanied by the soundtrack of her parents' fighting.

Maya thinks of all that Granny told her and she thinks about this George person, who is her grandfather, and wonders if she will like him, should they ever meet. 'It's in the lap of the gods,' Granny said, 'and you must be the one to decide if you want him

208

to know.'

There's been no mention of any visitors and for that Maya's very relieved. In her present emotional state she wouldn't be ready for any kind of confrontation, and she's only here for a few days, so maybe she can escape this time without any demands apart from meeting Henry. Granny was clear that she would like her to meet Henry.

'He reminds me of Jason when I first knew him,' she said. 'Jason wasn't sure of where he was going, an Honours graduate with nothing but a love of poetry and a passion for making things grow. Henry's rather like that. I think you might like him.'

Well, she's about to find out. Henry has been invited to what Leo calls the Ashes Party.

'Because Alice loved a party,' he is quick to explain, lest she thinks he's being crass. 'She would want us to be celebrating not weeping. You've brought her home, Maya. She wanted that so much.'

It's tragic that Granny felt that she couldn't come back but Maya can understand the complications. It would have been difficult to visit without explaining about her child, bringing him with her, and the shock when the family here saw the strong resemblance to his real father. It was wonderful to see her on her return in the summer. She was radiant, as if something great had been accomplished, and in those last weeks Maya was her constant companion, listening, comprehending, reassuring. And now she is here to carry out those last wishes.

Maya sets the box back on the table beside her bed and goes downstairs.

★ ★ ★

Leo is waiting apprehensively. It's one thing to talk about a celebration and quite another to bring it off with sensitivity. He enjoyed last evening with Maya. She's so like Alice that it hardly seems strange to have her here staying with him. She was utterly riveted by the photograph album, examining it eagerly, asking questions. She looked particularly closely at pictures of George when Leo explained who everyone was, and Leo remembered what Alice told him about the likeness between Adam and his father. Leo watched rather anxiously as Maya studied them but said nothing and it was only afterwards he realized that he'd been holding his breath. It was foolish of him to have shown her the album without removing those particular photos and he's been bracing himself ever since in case she should mention it.

He hears Henry arriving and is glad to be distracted from his anxiety. This must be a good day. It's another golden autumn day, perfect for their plan, but the big question is where the ashes are to be scattered.

'Hi, Henry,' Leo calls, just as Maya comes down the stairs. 'Come in and meet Maya.'

He makes the introductions, wondering what Alice would have made of this meeting between the young man she liked so much and her granddaughter. Maya and Henry smile at each other and say 'Hi.' Leo watches them sizing each other up, and wonders if they approve of what they see.

'Thanks for inviting me,' Henry says to her. 'I'm really grateful. I really liked Alice.'

Leo can see that this is a good thing to say. Maya nods, looking very slightly off balance.

'She liked you, too,' she answers. 'She wanted you to be here. Thanks for being so kind to her. She enjoyed herself so much.'

Leo can see that Maya is about to become emotional.

'So,' he says, before things get out of hand, 'we need to think about this. It's always difficult being practical at these moments but there's only one question really. Where the ashes are to be scattered.'

'Leo showed me all over the garden and the woodland and there are so many places to choose,' Maya tells Henry. 'And there's your little pavilion. It's really cute. She was so pleased with that and I can see why. But I was wondering,' she adds, turning to Leo, 'whether we should scatter them randomly or actually put them around a particular tree?'

Leo concentrates on her question, not wanting her to suspect that he already has his own idea of what should be done.

'Shall we go outside?' he suggests. 'If we walk around, somewhere might suggest itself naturally.'

He stands back so that Maya might go first and then follows Henry out. They pause just outside the door and Maya points at the hawthorn tree.

'How about there? Where you have tea outside in the summer? There's a photograph of you all there.'

Leo remembers the photograph: Alice standing beneath the branches watching Helen and George, newly married, smiling at the camera. Instinctively he shakes his head, and she nods at once, accepting his judgement, and they all move out together into the garden. Leo wonders if Maya is being polite, allowing him to choose. He knows where the ashes should be scattered, in the wildflower meadow, so that Alice will be remembered by anyone sitting in the pavilion, but he waits, hoping that they will all come to the same conclusion. He hangs behind them, seeing at what point the solemnity of the occasion draws back a little and they both begin to talk more naturally, exchanging information, beginning to learn each other a little. Finally their steps lead them past the arboretum, which is carefully scrutinized but ultimately rejected, to the meadow with the painted pavilion standing at the top. They walk along the path that skirts the field until they reach the pavilion and Maya looks around her.

'It has to be here, doesn't it?' she says. 'So that anyone could sit in the pavilion and think about her.'

Leo notes Henry's nod of agreement, his look of pride and pleasure, and smiles inwardly.

'It's the perfect place,' he agrees. 'Not least because Alice was so involved in the building of it and loved it so much.'

'Yes, she told me about it,' says Maya. 'It meant so much to her. So shall we scatter her ashes in the meadow? Or keep them in her little carved box and . . . bury them, or something.'

It's clear to both Leo and Henry that this last suggestion would not be Maya's choice and they both shake their heads.

'I think,' says Henry tentatively, 'that she should be free, in the meadow, amongst all the flowers.'

He glances at them anxiously, as if he might have spoken out of turn, but they both nod.

'I totally agree,' says Leo. 'Alice was a free spirit. She hated to be confined.'

'I'd go with that,' says Maya. 'Good, then. So when shall we do it? It needs to be special.'

'The moon's not quite full yet,' says Leo, 'but it's pretty special up here when the stars are coming out.

It's going to be a clear night. Shall we say half past six this evening?'

Henry politely waits to be included in the invitation and nods enthusiastically when Maya looks at him questioningly.

'That's settled, then,' says Leo. 'I'll provide the champagne. I'm going to take Maya down to the pub for lunch, Henry. Would you like to join us? Or are you working?'

'No,' answers Henry quickly. 'I kept today free in case . . . you know. In case. I'd love to come if . . . ' He glances at Maya, who smiles at him warmly.

'That would be great,' she says.

'Good,' says Leo. 'Let's get going, then.'

★ ★ ★

Henry follows Maya down the path, feeling as if something important is happening. He's never been quite so quickly attracted to a girl before. It's not just the physical reaction, although she is beautiful, but because she's easy to talk to, she has no sharp edges to make him wary of saying the wrong thing. But beneath that friendly, open confidence there's just a breath of vulnerability that touches him. He sees how close to the surface her emotions are, how much she is missing Alice, and he wants to comfort her, to protect her. He knows he's being a fool, but he doesn't care. She's here for only a few days and he wonders how he might take it forward. He's sure that Maya will come back to Long Orchard to see Leo, he has no doubt of that, but he'd like the opportunity to get to know her better. He would like his own personal contact with her, not to have to rely on Leo, but how? He can't ask her for her phone number and he can think of no way to make a move in this beginning of a friendship. For the first time, he wishes that he had prospects, a good job, a dazzling future, money. But somehow he doesn't quite believe that these things would necessarily impress Maya. She's the most unusual girl he's met, and he doesn't want to think that she'll simply vanish away out of his life in a few days' time. He can't understand this sense of urgency; it's completely wrong-footed him. He wonders if it's because she reminds him of Alice; he guesses that Alice must have looked a lot like Maya when she was young and he remembers thinking that if he had known Alice then, as Leo did, he would have been very attracted to her. She was ageless, like nobody he'd ever met before. And Maya is like her. It's rather as if he's known her for a long time, and perhaps it's because of this that his feelings are hurrying him along. Or perhaps it's because Alice has shown him how precious time is and that he shouldn't waste a moment of it. 'They are not long, the days of wine and roses.'

★ ★ ★

Maya is aware of Henry close behind her and she smiles secretly. He's really nice. Not pushy, or showing off, but kind and amusing, too, just like Granny said he was. To begin with she was determined not to be influenced by that, not wanting to feel as if she and Henry are being paired off. But as they've walked about, she's begun to tell him about her little cottage, how she wants to keep it, but doesn't quite know how yet, whilst she's at Cambridge. She told him how Granny worked as an interpreter in Oxford, how

214

fluent she was in Italian and French, which has inspired Maya's own love of languages. She confided that she would love to translate novels and he was really interested and impressed. Henry said rather sadly that he wasn't much good at anything except gardening.

'Like Grandpa Jason,' she answered him. 'He was the same. He was a landscape gardener and he quoted poetry all the time. I utterly loved him.'

Then she felt embarrassed and was rather glad that Leo caught them up and began to talk about the matter in hand.

Maya sighs with a kind of happiness mixed with her grief. She can understand why Granny wanted to come back here. Somehow she feels that she has come home, too. She wonders how it will work in the future; how often she might come to stay with Leo here at Long Orchard — and if Henry will be around. She would like to invite him to see the cottage, but can't quite see how she can do that without it being misunderstood. She has a little idea that she might test later, after the ceremony of the ashes. Perhaps Leo might like to visit her at the cottage, to see the orchard that Grandpa Jason loved, and to see the potager he made. She's already seen the beginnings of the potager here, and it might be possible to make the suggestion and then add casually that he might like to bring Henry along to see all the things Grandpa Jason achieved, and that she wants to be able to preserve. She'll need advice in the future and Leo is just the man to give it.

★ ★ ★

The night is clear as they walk in single file up to the pavilion. None of them wants to be the first to speak; each of them is thinking his or her own private thoughts. They reach the pavilion and go in. Henry places the bag containing the glasses and the champagne on the small wooden table but none of them sits down on the bench that is built against the back wall. Instead they stand, looking down the meadow, as if they are waiting for a signal, and Leo turns back and begins to unpack the bag, standing the glasses on the table and lifting out the bottle. The popping of the cork, the bubbles fizzing into the pretty crystal flutes, acts as a stimulant. Suddenly they are free of their restraint; they raise their glasses in a toast to Alice, to Granny, and they smile at one another, joined together in this special moment.

Then Maya puts down her glass and picks up the small carved box in both hands. She turns to look at Henry and they walk out together into the meadow. Opening the box, she gently, tenderly, shakes out the contents as they pass to and fro across the grass, whilst Leo stands watching them, lifting his glass again, saluting the magic of the evening and his memories.

23

Em sits at her favourite table in the café. She knows it was crazy to come back but some impulse drove her to check the B & Bs in the town and book a couple of nights. No use asking if the little flat might be available, she knew that. There's been a certain coolness between her and Bethany ever since the last visit here. Bethany is embarrassed for encouraging her old friend in her silly infatuation for her father-in-law and things have been just a mite strained. Nevertheless, Em still feels the least bit annoyed for having been cleverly out-manoeuvred by Bethany and that old bat, Jenny. This sudden impulse to return to Dartmouth was a requirement to get her own back: to try to see Leo again without any kind of outside interference.

And it was good to be back, to walk about the town again and along the Embankment, to watch the river traffic and the swooping gulls, and all the while hoping that she might bump into Leo: to see him come walking round a corner or to find him in a shop. It would have been very amusing to send a casual text to Bethany saying that she was down here again and that they'd met up, but Leo's text had crushed all those hopes.

Optimist she might be, but there was no need to read between the lines of his message; it was very clear.

Em sips at her mocha, smiling at the elderly man with his crossword, who waved when she came in and commented that it was good to see her again. The young mums are there as usual, and the good-looking guy who meets the blonde woman has just come in, glancing round, smiling in his friendly way. And here is the woman, hurrying in, looking a bit anxious. As she watches them embrace, Em wonders again about the relationship between them, but she is no longer interested in following Ruskin's advice, no longer engaged in planning her radio play. Too much like hard graft, and no real material to work on. At the same time, without the pretence at writing or her familiar emails to Bethany, it's not quite the same here. She loves it all but she feels slightly deflated and she's beginning to wish that she hadn't come back. She takes out her phone and begins to check her messages.

★ ★ ★

Sebastian can tell at once that his suspicions are well-founded and that Tessa is no longer in that wonderfully conspiratorial mood; no longer ready to engage with him, to flirt with him, and he feels disappointed. Since Liz left him, his pride has been damaged and Tessa's affection for him, the memories of the adoration she once felt for him, were consoling, a balm restoring his confidence. He's been thinking so much about her, remembering those days, way back, when she loved him, when he finally bit the bullet and asked her to marry him but, if he's totally honest, he knows that he was never one hundred per cent committed to Tessa, or to anyone; that he was always reluctant to take the final step.

And now, as he listens to her explaining that she can't leave Giles, that she loves him and her children, Sebastian knows that deep down he's been expecting this. Tessa is too loyal, too conventional, to step away

218

from her marriage and even as she talks, trying to be kind, to make him understand, he knows that nothing will change her mind. He decides to let her off lightly, to bring this embarrassment to a close, but before he can make a dignified exit, Tessa finishes her coffee and stands up.

'I must get back,' she says. ''Bye, Sebastian.'

She bends to kiss him lightly on the cheek and hurries out, and he's left, feeling a prat and not knowing quite what to do. Glancing round to see if anybody has witnessed the encounter, he sees the young woman in the corner, watching him. She has an odd expression on her face, a kind of humorous sympathy, as if she knows what's happened and understands how he feels. He responds instantly and instinctively. He shrugs, lifting his hands in a helpless gesture and makes a face.

'I think I've been stood up,' he says.

She laughs — actually she's very attractive — and nods.

'Me, too,' she says.

He makes a gesture that says, 'May I join you?' and she nods again at once.

Getting up, he moves to her table, and then pauses.

'Shall I order us some more coffee?' he suggests.

This is a test question. If she says yes, then he knows he's in with a chance.

'A mocha,' she says. 'Thank you. My name's Emily.'

'I'm Sebastian,' he says. 'How very nice to meet you properly at last.'

★ ★ ★

The elderly man watches the exchange, amused by it all. He's seen the blonde woman go out and noted that there's an air of finality about her exit, and now he has no qualms about listening to the relationship that is developing at the next table. Apparently, they both live in London. She works with an advertising agency and he is at the MOD. They're getting along like a house on fire as he folds up his newspaper and prepares to leave.

Charlie, the owner of the café, is coming in as he reaches the door. He smiles, holds the door wide.

'How's the book coming on?' he asks.

Charlie knows his secret but has promised not to tell.

'Very well, thank you, Charlie,' he answers. 'Lots of good ideas. In cafés there are always stories if you have the ears to hear and the eyes to see them.'

* * *

Hurrying towards the car park, Tessa almost bumps into Will, who is staring into the window of an art gallery.

'Steady the Buffs,' he exclaims, catching her arm. 'Are you OK?'

He can tell that she isn't — she looks as if she's escaping from something or someone — and he turns with her, walking beside her, still holding her arm.

'I'm fine,' she says. 'Honestly. I've just been saying goodbye to an old friend in Bayards.'

Will nods. 'Sebastian?' he suggests gently.

'Yes,' she says. 'Yes, I think it might have been getting a bit out of hand, if you see what I mean. There was nothing, really, but you know how it can be?'

220

'Oh, yes,' says Will, remembering a certain young woman called Isobel. 'I know exactly how it can be. None of us is proof against it. Look, let's go into the Castle and have some coffee. This is my first solo trip since the operation and I need to celebrate.'

He sits down while she goes to the bar to order coffee, wondering if it were rather tactless to bring her here, where she'd come with Sebastian on that morning back in May. Or perhaps it is necessary. As she sits down opposite he can see that she's thinking the same thing.

'You knew, didn't you?' she asks. 'You and Bea. That morning that we came in here?'

'I think we suspected that it was just a bit more than a casual encounter,' he agrees. 'But we remembered that he was an old friend . . .'

'I suppose that was the attraction,' Tessa says wretchedly. 'Being able to talk about anything and everything.'

'And exciting, too, when you've shared love?'

She looks at him and quite unexpectedly she begins to smile, and then to laugh.

'What a dangerous man you are, Will Rainbird,' she says. 'And what a comfort. Yes, of course, it was sexy, flirting with him just a little bit, while all the time . . .'

'All the time you were safe behind your marriage vows.' He grins at her. 'I hope you know that there's a word for women like you?'

To his relief she laughs even more, and he sees that she's passed the stormy emotional stage of saying goodbye to Sebastian and is in calmer waters.

'Giles is being very good about it,' she admits. 'It was terrible, telling him. And then telling Sebastian, too. Although,' she adds, almost spitefully, 'I don't

221

suppose he'll take much time to get over it.'

'But that's all to the good,' says Will peaceably. 'He needs to accept that it's over and to leave you alone. And stop sending you texts.'

She glances at him. 'Did it show?'

He begins to laugh. 'Oh, darling Tessa. Have you never heard the old expression, 'Love and a cough cannot be hid'?'

'No,' she says, crossly. 'I feel even more of a prat now.'

'Join the club,' says Will. 'So Giles doesn't know you were meeting Sebastian?'

'Good God, no,' she says, alarmed. 'You won't tell him, will you? He wouldn't understand that I just needed to do it properly. To finish it face to face, so that Sebastian really believed it.'

Will can understand that.

'And how did he react?'

She makes a face. 'I didn't give him much time to react. I was all wound up for it and I think he guessed. After all, it was never really going anywhere. I think I was just a consolation to his wounded pride after his divorce.'

'Put it down to experience,' says Will, as their coffee arrives. 'Time to let it go and move on.'

'You won't tell anyone that I met him, will you?' she asks again. 'Not even Bea.'

He shakes his head. 'I promise I shan't say a word.'

'I'm sorry to involve you in it,' she says. 'It's not fair to make you promise, especially when I know how close you and Bea are. Sorry, Will.'

'Oh, I can keep a secret,' he promises. 'Good grief, you don't think I tell Bea everything, do you? So tell me, did you leave Sebastian in the café? Yes? Well then,

222

when we've finished our coffee I'll walk you to your car just in case he's still around. Then there won't be any more complications. And then I suggest that you extend your journey to somewhere else.'

She looks puzzled. 'Why?'

'Because then, should Bea or Giles wonder where you've been you can tell them you went to Blackpool Sands or Totnes, without endangering your immortal soul. Tell the truth but not all of it. Bea knows that I'm here, you see, so we need to cover our tracks.'

Tessa looks at him in admiration. 'You know, I'm beginning to think you might have been a bit of a player,' she says.

Will beams at her, pleased to see her back on form.

'But why do you put it in the past tense?' he asks blandly. 'Drink up and we'll get you out of here.'

★ ★ ★

Henry sits down on the edge of a planter outside the farm shop and looks at Maya's text. He's sorry to say goodbye to her but she's shown that she hopes that their friendship will continue, given him her phone number, though she's careful to emphasize that there's nothing too serious here. He understands. She's very young and has no family in this country at the moment, but she's very self-contained, confident, and he respects that and has agreed to stay in touch without looking too keen. There's a plan that Leo might go to Oxford to see the cottage and the place where Alice's ashes have been scattered, and it's been suggested that Henry might go with him, but Henry has his own ideas about a visit.

It's not that he doesn't want to go with Leo — who

has hinted that he might be glad of his company — but that he's thinking that the moment might come when he would like his growing friendship with Maya to be moved out from this feeling of it being arranged or approved by their elders. He's well aware that he's been caught off guard by his attraction to Maya and he knows he must play it cool.

Perhaps a visit to Cambridge once the university term is under way might be a good move, but meanwhile he's encouraged by this text from her saying that it was great to meet him, with several emojis — a train, a suitcase — indicating that she's on her way home.

He thinks carefully about a response to this but decides to play it safe and simply sends:

Have a good journey.

He's beginning to realize how complicated relationships can be.

★   ★   ★

Maya is very quiet on the journey to the station, and Leo glances at her from time to time, wondering if he should try to break the silence. But it is she who suddenly speaks, taking him by surprise.

'I've been thinking, Leo,' she says, staring straight ahead. 'I don't want to go back without saying something. It's something Granny told me. You know it, but I know that you don't know that I know.'

'That sounds slightly complicated,' he says, trying for a light note. 'I think you need to tell me.' Although deep down he can guess what is coming and he braces himself for it.

'It's about George,' she says. 'Granny explained what happened between her and George all those years ago. She told me that he's my dad's father but nobody knows except you. And, of course, Grandpa Jason. She didn't come back to Long Orchard for all those years because Dad looks so much like George. And now I've seen the photographs I can see what she means. She wanted me to know because she said that one day it might be important.'

Her voice falters a little and Leo wonders if he should stop the car but is afraid to interrupt the flow of her thoughts.

'I can sort of see what she means by that and I don't have a problem with George being my grandfather,' Maya continues, 'though I could never love him like I loved Grandpa Jason. But I'm not quite sure where to go from there. She said that one day it might all become clear but that I shouldn't worry about it.'

'It's very hard,' says Leo, after a moment, when he's sure she's finished speaking, 'for you to have the burden of it now, rather than your father or George, but I can understand what was in her mind. Life has many twists and turns and she wanted you to be ready for any eventuality. She could see no reason to tell your father. What could be achieved by it? Only pain and damage all round, but there might come a time in the future when you and George might be able to speak about it. That there might be some value or comfort in it. I can't quite see how, but I'm sure, if it is meant to be, it will be revealed at some moment when the time is right.'

He knows his answer is inadequate but she glances at him and gives a little smile.

'Thanks, old Lion,' she says. 'Just as long as you're there.'

He can hardly speak — emotion almost closes up

his throat — but he stretches out his hand and gives hers a quick clasp.

'Always,' he says.

He drives into the station and they go out on to the platform together. The train draws in and they look at each other, slightly embarrassed, not quite knowing how to say goodbye. But she drops her bags and puts both arms around him, hugging him close, then she picks up her bags again and climbs on to the train. He waves to her until the train vanishes round the bend in the track, and walks back to the car. He sits for a moment, and then drives away out of the town, heading home.

★   ★   ★

Will puts away the chessboard, smiling to himself, having beaten Leo for the first time in several weeks. He could see that his old friend's mind wasn't fully on the game and he'd exploited it ruthlessly. Bea, coming in to lay the table for supper, looks at him sharply.

'What are you grinning at?' she asks.

Will laughs out loud, then looks a bit sheepish.

'It's that conversation we were having about young Henry,' he admits. 'The way he's been going around with that look on his face ever since Maya went back. You know, that 'Ah, 'tis love, 'tis love' expression. The poor boy's got it bad, though he's trying very hard not to show it.'

'I'm sorry we didn't get to meet her,' says Bea.

'So am I,' says Will. 'I'd like to see the kind of girl who can knock Henry sideways. He's got so many of them hanging round him he's usually quite impervious. But I can see that it wasn't the moment to bring her over to meet four complete strangers. She was only here for a few days and it wasn't that sort of social occasion, was it? I'm sure she'll be over next time.'

'So there's going to be a next time, is there?' asks Bea.

'From what Leo was saying just now I think it's an absolute certainty. Apparently there's a plan for him and Henry to drive up and visit her cottage. I think she's taking on Alice's mantle and wanting to be one of the family, which will help Leo with his grieving. I suspect he's been much sadder than he's letting on and I think this whole visit has helped him to come to terms with it.'

'And talking of coming to terms with things,' says Bea, 'Tessa seems to be coming out of that mad moment with Sebastian. Did you notice that she seemed much more like her old self when she came in this afternoon?'

Will keeps his back to her, determined to give nothing away.

'I wonder if Giles found out and they've managed to talk about it,' he says casually. 'I agree that she was very relaxed earlier. I suspect that he suggested this visit to Cornwall to help things along. They need time together alone. I think it's a great idea.'

'And Henry's left to look after Bodger?'

Will nods. 'And us,' he adds, grinning.

Bea snorts. 'That'll be the day. He'll be round for all his meals, you mark my words.'

'And you know you'll love every minute of it,' he answers. 'So now I'm on a winning streak, how about a game of Scrabble after supper? Best out of three games and the loser does the washing up.'

Leo leaves Will and Bea and sets off down the lane, but he pauses for a moment outside his own gate before walking on to the village, down the steps and across the beach to the sea's edge. He sits down, drawing his knees up and folding his arms around them. He thinks of Alice: how they sat here together as children — 'We'll always be together, won't we, old Lion?' — and again on the eve of Helen's wedding. And finally, when they met for the last time here and he welcomed her back. So many memories.

Now, at last, he has fulfilled his promise and he is at peace: Alice is home again and they will always be together. He watches the harvest moon, immense, golden, rising above the horizon, throwing a path of shimmering gold across the water almost to his feet. The tide has turned and, as the waves rush in over the sand, the only sound is the eternal murmuring of the restless sea.

We do hope that you have enjoyed
reading this large print book.

Did you know that all of our titles
are available for purchase?

We publish a wide range of high
quality large print books including:
Romances, Mysteries, Classics
General Fiction
Non Fiction and Westerns

Special interest titles available in
large print are:
The Little Oxford Dictionary
Music Book, Song Book
Hymn Book, Service Book

Also available from us courtesy of
Oxford University Press:
Young Readers' Dictionary
(large print edition)
Young Readers' Thesaurus
(large print edition)

For further information or a free
brochure, please contact us at:
Ulverscroft Large Print Books Ltd.,
The Green, Bradgate Road, Anstey,
Leicester, LE7 7FU, England.
Tel: (00 44) 0116 236 4325
Fax: (00 44) 0116 234 0205

Other titles published by Ulverscroft:

THE GARDEN HOUSE

Marcia Willett

After the death of her father, El moves into his home just outside Tavistock in Devon. Fresh out of university she questions what it is she really wants from life. Although her childhood friend, Will, is there to help her through her grief she soon realises there were things her father was hiding from her . . .

Jules is also mourning Martin, but they thought best to keep their relationship secret, and now she must grieve entirely alone. All she has to remember her love are the memories of their time spent at The Garden House — where they met, fell in love and where their secret affair will inevitably be uncovered.

As El and Will begin to piece together her father's secrets they bring them closer to both Jules and a truth that is difficult to face.

REFLECTIONS

Marcia Willett

After her husband dies, Cara no longer wishes to live in their London home. On impulse, she sells it and goes to stay with her brother in Salcombe, Devon. There, she looks back at her life and reflects on the choices that have led her to this moment.

Cosmo has also escaped — temporarily — from his life in the city, finding the south-west an appealing fit, especially when he meets a local girl, Amy. But is he being entirely truthful about what he's left behind?

Just out of uni, Sam is set to follow in his naval father's footsteps. His future is secure — but he feels cast adrift and an impartial new friend could be just the thing he needs. Forging a bond across the generations, can he and Cara help each other find the way to a new chapter?

HOMECOMINGS

Marcia Willett

At the end of the row of fishermen's cottages by the harbour's edge, stands an old granite house.

First it belonged to Ned's parents; then Ned dropped anchor here after a life at sea and called it home. His nephew Hugo moved in too, swapping London for the small Cornish fishing village where he'd spent so many happy holidays.

It's a refuge — and now other friends and relations are being drawn to the house by the sea. Among them is Dossie, who's lonely after her parents died and her son remarried. And Jamie, who's coming home after more than a year, since his career in the RAF was abruptly cut short.

As newcomers arrive and old friends reunite, secrets are uncovered, relationships are forged and tested, and romance is kindled.